The cowboy blocked the sun with his six-foot-plus self.

"You okay?"

She looked back at her trailer, her lungs tight. "I'm fine. And hopefully, all my supplies are, too." What would she tell the restoration committee?

The truth—that some cowboy had totaled her vehicle and overturned her trailer.

He made a visual sweep of the overturned trailer behind her. "I'll round up a couple of fellas to help me right this thing." He lifted his Stetson, revealing caramel-colored hair, and wiped the sweat off his forehead. "Hope you don't have anything fragile in there."

She fought to keep her frustration—and anxiety—in check. "Just glass."

"Like the kind they use in windows?"

"Yes, why?"

He scratched his jaw. "You wouldn't be from Leaded Pane Restoration, would you?"

So he knew about the church, then? And about the company she'd bid against. "No. I'm a private contractor and artist." She donned her most professional smile. "Faith Nichols."

He continued to study her, expression stiff, as the two shook hands, his grip strong. "Drake Owens. Good to meet you."

Why did she get the feeling that wasn't exactly true?

Jennifer Slattery is a writer and speaker who's addressed women's and church groups across the nation. As the founder of Wholly Loved Ministries, she and her team help women rest in their true worth and live with maximum impact. When not writing, Jennifer loves spending time with her adult daughter and hilarious husband. Visit her online at jenniferslatterylivesoutloud.com to learn more or to book her for your next women's event.

Book by Jennifer Slattery

Love Inspired

Restoring Her Faith

Visit the Author Profile page at Harlequin.com.

Restoring
Her Faith

Jennifer Slattery

Recycling programs
for this product may
not exist in your area.

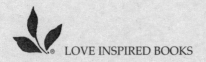 LOVE INSPIRED BOOKS

ISBN-13: 978-1-335-53920-5

Restoring Her Faith

www.Harlequin.com

Printed in U.S.A.

Now faith is the substance of things hoped for, the evidence of things not seen.
—*Hebrews* 11:1

I dedicate this story to my artistic daughter, Ashley.

Acknowledgments

I want to give a huge thanks to my agent, Tamela Hancock Murray, for all the ways she's guided and encouraged me. I also want to thank my husband for listening to my ideas and sentences, paragraphs and pages as I read them for the umpteenth time. Shannon Taylor Vannatter, thank you for all the constructive feedback, encouragement and prayers you've offered over the years, and Mindy Obenhaus and Renee Ryan, thank you for all the guidance you provided as I worked through this story. I want to thank Architectural Glass Arts for teaching me how to work with stained glass, answering my questions and sharing your cool restoration stories! Finally, thank You to my Savior, the author of fun, romance and creativity.

Chapter One

The long, deserted road felt much too similar to one Faith had taken decades before, with all her belongings crammed in a pair of tattered suitcases. Hopefully Sage Creek would be nothing like her experience in Alpine, back when she'd been a gawky, metal-mouthed kid in desperate need of a friend.

She'd received taunting and rejection instead.

Her cell phone rang, and she glanced at the screen. It was her best friend, Toni. As a fellow artist fighting to survive Austin's competitive market, she understood Faith in a way few others did.

She answered through her Bluetooth. "Hey, girl. What's up?"

"Girls' night out this Friday. Bahn mi French fries, baby!"

"Sounds fun but can't. I'm on my way to that contract job I told you about. I'm just over fif-

teen miles out. With no sign of civilization, except the occasional longhorn, in sight."

"You make Sage Creek sound so appealing."

Faith glanced at her wobbly trailer through
her rearview mirror, packed with, she hoped,
everything she'd need to restore Trinity Faith's
historic stained glass windows, which had decorated the church since its founding. "Let's just
say I haven't had the best experience with small-
town Texans."

"Not all ranching communities measure a person's worth based on how well they bake a casserole. Besides, those people didn't hire you to
make friends."

"True." She was going to, hopefully, get some
media exposure, enough to salvage her career.
If she, and whoever else she'd be working with,
pulled this job off well, the church stood a good
chance of receiving historical status. "Depending on how this deal turns out, I may even be
able to get Jeremy Pratt from *Lone Star Gems*
to write a feature article on me."

"Wow. Just a mention in that magazine would
for sure get folks' attention. But a full story?
That'd put your name on the map for sure."

She gripped her steering wheel with both
hands as something black—a tire?—came barreling toward her in the opposite lane, while a
red pickup screeched past, throwing sparks.

She screamed and slammed on her brakes. Her

trailer tugged right, then left as the oncoming tire rammed into her front end. It bounced off, flying ten feet into the adjacent field.

Smoke seeped from beneath her hood as she veered onto the shoulder, and the acrid stench of burning rubber pricked her nose.

"Faith, you okay?"

"I…" Her throat felt scratchy. What had happened? "Can I call you back? I was just hit by a…a flying tire. The front of my car is smoking."

Her supplies! She shot a glance to her trailer—lying on its side—behind her. She groaned and closed her eyes.

Faith pressed trembling fingers to her temples. Now what? All her sheets of specially ordered glass, potentially shattered. She didn't have time to order new. And what about the damage done to her car? Fighting the urge to hyperventilate, she focused on her breathing—in through her nose, out through her mouth. In, out…

Did Sage Creek even have a mechanic? Probably one that charged outsiders ten times what they should. Through her rearview window, she watched a tall, broad-shouldered cowboy step out of his now lopsided truck. Dressed in faded jeans and a Stetson, the man had to be at least six foot five and was built like a linebacker.

She swallowed, checking the road in either direction. There wasn't another vehicle, tractor or farmhouse in sight. No one but Mr. Tall Muscular Stranger who, at this moment, was heading her way.

She caught a glimpse of herself in her sideview mirror. Olive complexion washed out, eyes more pupil than gray, chestnut hair tumbling out of her messy ponytail in a frazzled mess—like she felt. All giving her the appearance of a defenseless city girl who knew more about complementary colors than how to manage nearly totaled cars.

Suddenly the cowboy stood beside her door, blocking the sun. Making her acutely aware of her tiny five-foot, one-hundred-pound frame in comparison.

A faint dusting of scruff covered his square jaw. His green eyes, framed by thick, caramel-colored lashes, latched on to hers. "You okay?" The man bore a striking resemblance to Chris Hemsworth.

"I'm fine." She got out and marched toward her overturned trailer. "And hopefully, all my supplies are, too." Insurance would pay for the damage, right? But that could take a while, and her credit cards were maxed. What would she tell the restoration committee?

The truth—that some reckless, broad-shouldered cowboy's tire had smashed into her car.

He made a visual sweep of her vehicle, then the overturned trailer behind her. "Sorry about this." He swept a muscled arm toward her caved-in front end. "Seems my mechanic friend forgot to tighten my lug nuts. I felt that right wheel wobbling. Was about to pull off."

He should've done that a couple miles back. At least her overturned trailer wasn't dented. That was a good sign, right? Hopefully her careful packing had kept the glass from breaking. She was afraid to open the doors for fear of everything falling out.

"Let me give you my insurance information." He pulled out a faded leather wallet and flipped it open. "I'll call a buddy tow truck driver, see if I can get him out here. Except his phone might be off, being Sunday and all. Got something I can write with?"

She nodded and returned to her car for a pen and slip of paper. She handed both over.

The brim of his hat shadowed most of his face. "Where you headed?"

"Not much farther. A town called Sage Creek."

"You got family here?"

She shook her head. "Going for a job."

"Who you working for?"

Strange question, and not one she felt comfortable answering. "I don't mean to be rude, but that's your business how?"

He gave a one-shoulder shrug. "Figured I might know the fella." He adjusted his hat, revealing brown hair, cut short and neat, streaked with blond. "Or gal, whatever. I could give you a lift to the place, if you want. If I can't get ahold of my buddy with the tow truck, I mean."

"If you must know, I'm here to restore some stained glass windows."

He scratched his jaw, head angled. "You wouldn't be from Leaded Pane Restoration, would you? To work on Trinity Faith? 'Cept…" He gazed down the road. "…you're coming from the wrong way."

So he knew about the church, then? And about the company she'd bidden against. "No. I'm a private contractor and artist. From Austin." She straightened, donned her most professional smile. "Faith Nichols."

"Drake Owens."

His stiff expression didn't sit right with her. "You got a problem with that?"

"You're sure you're supposed to be here? On the job, I mean?"

She frowned. "Why wouldn't I be?"

"I don't remember the team hiring on extra folks. Seeing as I'm the contractor overseeing the job, seems someone would've said something to me about you coming."

"Yeah, well, you weren't the one to hire me."

"We've been working with Leaded Pane Restoration for going on three generations. Don't see why the committee would be looking to change that now."

Great. So not only was she starting this project

with broken supplies, but she'd be working for a man who clearly didn't want her here.

Fingers pressed to her temples, Faith focused on taking slow, even breaths. Her hands, still slick with sweat from her death grip on her steering wheel, trembled. That tire could've shattered her windshield, maybe even caused her to lose control of her vehicle.

"I'll get some buddies out here to help lift your trailer." Drake pulled a phone from his back pocket. "Let me make a few calls."

"Me, too." She held up the slip of paper on which he'd written his insurance information, and returned to her car. Fifteen minutes later, two trucks, both driven by cowboys, one wearing a straw hat, the other a tattered gray one, arrived.

The sheriff was coming, right? Maybe she should phone again? She'd give him ten more minutes.

Drake faced his "buddies," as he called them. He tipped his hat as they sauntered over. "Hey. Thanks for coming. And for bringing my dad's truck."

The taller of the two, a guy with dark hair and dark eyes, offered her a brisk nod. "No problem. So long's I'm back by the time they start cutting into the pies." He chuckled and addressed Faith. "I hear you're the gal hired on by the cultural committee."

She looked at Drake, who appeared to be

scrutinizing her, then back to his friends. "That's me."

"Well, now." The guy clamped a hand on Drake's shoulder. "This isn't the best way to treat one of Sage Creek's honored guests. It's hotter than a midsummer fire pit today."

Drake crouched beside the trailer. "You fellas ready?" His friends joined him, and after a few grunts and groans, they'd righted the thing.

"Thank you." Holding her breath, she unlocked the dead bolt and slowly opened the double doors. She groaned and squeezed her eyes shut. At least three sheets of glass were fractured—three of her most expensive pieces.

"Oh, man." Drake swiped a hand over his face. "I'll take care of this. I'm so sorry."

She needed to be at the job site first thing tomorrow morning, with less than a month to complete the project. With absolutely no wiggle room. Did Artisan's Glass have any extra sheets on hand? If not, how soon would they be able to get some in?

They'd probably charge her the freight fee.

"Listen, I'll—"

She raised a hand, then called her glass supplier. The phone rang half a dozen times. No answer. Lovely. She'd keep trying until she reached them.

The hum of an engine approached, then slowed. She glanced over her shoulder. The sheriff. Good. Hopefully this meant she'd soon be done here and recovering in her nice, air-conditioned hotel room.

Drake's phone rang as she relayed the details of the accident to the officer. She paused to listen.

"I know, and I don't blame you for that." Drake rubbed the back of his neck. "But we're kind of in a bind here."

He explained what had happened. "Both our vehicles need to be towed. I'll drive my dad's truck until mine gets fixed. When do you think you could get out here?" He gave a low whistle. Lowering his phone, he turned to Faith. "My friend with the tow truck—today's his day off."

"And?"

"He said he'd come out, but it might be a while."

"How long are you talking?"

"Didn't say. I suspect after the church picnic."

She closed her eyes and pinched the bridge of her nose. Perfect. What was she supposed to do now? Call someone from Austin? That'd take hours.

"That glass that broke… I'm going to need to replace it."

Drake nodded. "I'm sure my insurance company will cover it."

"I mean ASAP. I'll probably have to have it rush ordered."

"Okay. I'll make sure it's taken care of."

In other words, take him at his word. But what choice did she have? At least she had witnesses.

"Tell you what…" Drake's dark-haired friend scratched his jaw. "I've got some thick cord in the back of my truck. Bet we could rig this vehicle to our trailer hitch and pull it into town." He looked at Drake. "Leave Billy to tow yours whenever he gets to it. And you could pull her trailer with your pop's truck."

The officer clamped a hand on Drake's shoulder. "Good thinking, boys."

Faith bit her lip. Let a couple of strangers haul her car? But…they were friends with the town sheriff. And it was hot. Not to mention she was starving. And thirsty. "I, uh, I guess. But I'd like to grab my bike."

The men's eyes shifted to the top of her automobile, where her mountain bike remained secured, thankfully unharmed.

"No problem. I'll load it in the bed of my dad's truck." Drake began unlatching the clamps on her top-mounted rack, his shoulder muscles straining beneath his cotton T-shirt.

The officer tore off a sheet of paper from a pad and handed it to Faith. A blank report form. "Fill this out." He handed another page to Drake. "You, too."

Drake shifted a few steps back to use her trunk as a writing table.

The officer followed. "How's your dad doing?" He wiped the sweat off his forehead using his shirtsleeve. "Any talk of selling his place?"

"Nope. Not a lick."

"People been pestering him, though?"

"Doesn't matter. I have no intention of letting those land-hungry weasels wear my folks down."

The officer studied Drake. "I admire you, boy. How hard you're trying to save your parents' ranch and all. Just be careful your stubbornness doesn't land everyone in a mess they can't get out of."

A tendon in Drake's jaw twitched. "That property's been in our family for going on six generations. I intend to make sure that doesn't change."

Faith cleared her throat to interrupt their conversation, or perhaps remind them she was there. She handed her form to the officer.

"Y'all finished?" He closed his notepad and slid it into his front pocket.

His radio crackled, and he moved aside to answer. Sounded like another accident somewhere. "Ten-four. I'll head there now." He clipped his radio back on his shoulder mount, then turned to Drake. "Think you can give her a lift into town? There's a fender-bender out on Harrison I got to attend to."

"Sure. No problem." He flicked his dark-haired friend's arm. "Y'all can follow whenever you get this contraption secured." Then he turned to Faith with a grin that made her stomach do an odd flip. For reasons she didn't care to entertain. "Where you staying?"

"The Cedar View Inn, just outside of town."

"Ah. Mr. Johnson's place. Great guy. He'll treat you good—best lodging within a forty-mile radius."

Also known as the only hotel around. As to how nice the rooms were, she wasn't holding her breath. Though her breathing did stall whenever the blue-eyed cowboy caught her gaze.

Not good. Not good at all.

Chapter Two

Drake Owens glanced at the frazzled city girl, dressed like one of those granola types, sitting in the passenger's seat beside him. Chestnut hair fell over her shoulders in long, loose waves. Gray eyes shadowed by deeply furrowed brows hinted that a spitfire lingered just below her polite smiles and thank-yous.

Pretty enough to jumble a man's head, if he wasn't careful. Drake never had that problem with the folks from Leaded Pane.

His phone rang. His headset answered. "Hey-lo."

"You called?" It was Elizabeth, his sister.

"Just making sure y'all made it down to the lake all right," Drake said. "That my rascally sons didn't give you and Mom too much trouble." At three and a half and six years old, those two could be quite a handful. His mom had always managed to keep them wrangled well enough…

until Dad's accident. Now she spent most of her time caring for him. Luckily, Drake's sister had stepped in to help nanny, almost full-time. Otherwise he would've had to back out of the restoration project.

"Oh, your boys were fine. Getting Dad into the truck was another story."

"The picnic will be good for him. He needs to get out of the house. Mom, too."

"I know. Now if I could somehow get him to socialize a little... He's been tight-lipped all day."

More like all month, not that Drake could blame him. That fall from the barn loft had stolen more than his mobility. He'd lost his independence, ability to provide for his family, to do what he'd always loved...

If he lost the ranch, too...

Drake refused to let that happen.

"William!" Drake's sister called out to his youngest. "Get that out of your mouth!" With a sigh, she returned to the phone. "Got to go. See you in a few?"

"Yep." Soon as he dropped his feisty little friend off.

Not that he could blame her for her sour mood. He'd just ruined her afternoon in a big way. To think that if he'd stayed out at Mr. Farmer's for ten more minutes, he might've avoided the accident altogether... But he'd been too wrapped up thinking about his parents' financial issues. As a result, he'd totaled her car, and nearly sent her trailer flying with who knows how many thousands of dollars' worth of stained glass.

Speaking of…why was she here instead of the guys from Leaded Pane? As a family-owned business from Northeast Texas, they understood the importance of maintaining the flavor of a place. Not so with city folks, like this princess sitting next to him. They always seemed compelled to force their progress on everyone else.

As if a town couldn't make its own decisions.

That church held way too much history, personal and otherwise, to let some city girl botch things up.

An image filled his mind of his wife standing at the altar. She'd looked beautiful dressed in a white lace gown that hugged her soft curves, the Garden of Eden mural covering the wall behind her. The deep green in the leaves had provided a beautiful contrast to her strawberry-blond highlights and peachy complexion. Her blue eyes were so full of life—until cancer stole that from her.

Though he no longer felt the sharp sting of grief, he would always hold tight to the memories of all they'd shared. A good deal of them in that small country church.

He slowed as he neared the Cedar View Inn. "How long you been in the restoration business?"

Her gaze met his, held it long enough to spike

his pulse. But then her cheeks flushed and she looked away. "A while."

She was such a tight-lipped little thing. Because she was quiet or lacked the experience to do the job? Then again, she might still be shaken up from the accident. Or spitting mad. "Bet you been all over the country, huh?"

She gave a slight shrug and focused on the single-story, metal-roofed motel in front of her. He eyed her trendy silk tank, long flowing skirt and strappy white sandals. Had city girl been expecting something fancier?

"Listen, about your car…" He cast her a sideways glance, momentarily distracted by the soft curve of her cheek. "I'll make sure it gets fixed up right, and as quick as possible."

"I'd appreciate that." Her tone held a hint of a bite.

The truck jolted as he hit a pothole, before pulling up to the cement parking bumper. "This is it." His was the only vehicle in the lot. "Except…looks like Mr. Johnson, the hotel owner, isn't here."

"What does that mean?"

"There's no one to check you in at the moment. The place doesn't get enough business for front desk staff."

"Oh." She frowned. "Mind if I call him? Before you leave, I mean?"

Her vulnerable tone drew Drake to her in the most inconvenient way. "Sure."

He waited, engine humming, while she rummaged through her purse and pulled out a folded slip of paper. Looked like a printed-out email.

"Thanks." Phone to her ear a moment later, she sighed. "Voice mail." She pinched the bridge of her nose. "Hello, this is Faith Nichols, I spoke to you last week. I have a reservation…" She closed her eyes and rubbed her forehead. "For tomorrow. But I was hoping you might have a vacancy tonight." She left her number, then dropped her phone back into her purse.

She leaned back against her seat, obviously completely flustered.

This had been quite a day for her. Because of him. "Most likely the owner's at the church picnic. I wouldn't expect him back until…" Drake placed his hand on his gearshift, prepared to reverse the truck and trailer. "You hungry?"

"Excuse me?"

You would've thought he'd asked her to eat a worm, the way her head jerked toward him. He was merely trying to be friendly. He couldn't exactly leave her here. "Figured maybe you'd like to come to the picnic."

She scraped her teeth across her bottom lip, then gave a slow nod. "I might as well."

"All right then. Give me a minute to turn this thing around." He reached for the door handle, then paused. "I figure you'll want to leave your gear here, instead of having us drag it all over the place?"

"That'd probably be best, thanks. Just let me put a lock on the wheels. The doors are already dead-bolted."

"What about your bike?"

She glanced around. "I'll chain it to that tree over there."

"Sounds good." He swung his truck around, maneuvered her trailer into a parking slot and unhitched it. Less than five minutes later, he was driving down the local road.

"Maybe you should drop me off at the mechanic's so I can check on my car."

"I got Mike's number, if you want to call. Though I suspect he'll phone you soon as he knows something."

"Mike?"

"He owns the repair shop. Though he's probably at the picnic, too." Drake slowed as they entered town. "Most everybody is. Few folks will turn down a free plate of fried chicken."

"I see." Her eyes tracked the single-story storefronts, which probably looked run-down and archaic to a city girl like her.

But to him, the simple brick exteriors, the signs that could use fresh coats of paint and the arching windows with peeling trim, were rife with memories. While so many other towns had chosen to replace the flavor of their area with the new and shiny, Sage Creek's residents valued history over glitz. For that he was grateful.

"I suppose that café over there is closed, as well?" She pointed to Wilma's Kitchen, the only full-service diner in town.

He eyed the dark windows, shaded by a sun-bleached green awning.

"All right." Faith held her purse close. "The picnic will be fine. Thank you." She paused. "You'll bring me back to the hotel later?"

"Sure thing."

That woman was as stiff as a hitching post, and clearly ready to bail from his truck at the first opportunity. Hopefully a plate of fried chicken would relax her some, and come tomorrow, at the job site, they could start over. On better footing. Otherwise things could turn troublesome real quick.

As she stepped from Drake's truck, faces turned Faith's way, eyebrows raised. As if she held a giant sign that shouted, "Out-of-towner. Not one of us."

Just like in middle school. Not that it mattered what these people thought of her.

She needed to stay focused on why she was here.

Loading up their plates, men, women and children crowded around three rectangular tables set end to end. Others sat on folding chairs or blankets spread out on the grass in the shade of giant oak trees. Laughter and the scents of baked berry pies and beef stew floated on the air, making her stomach grumble.

"Daddy!" A blond, chubby-cheeked little boy with bright eyes ran toward Drake. He held out a glass jar. "Look."

Was he married? She glanced at his bare ring finger.

He grinned, dropped to one knee and wrapped an arm around the boy. "Whatcha got there? A toad?"

The child's head bobbed. "His name's Toady. Can I keep him?"

"He's got a name already, does he?" Drake's grin crinkled the skin around his eyes.

"Figured you'd be more pleased with his catch than I was." A curvy woman with long blond hair came toward him. His wife? Strange how the thought bothered Faith. "I suppose now's as good a time as any to tell you what your other son's been doing."

Drake ruffled the child's hair, then stood. "Making mud pies down by the lake?"

"Close enough." The lady turned to Faith, as if seeing her for the first time. "Hey." Her gaze shifted from her to Drake, then back again. "I'm Elizabeth, Drake's sister."

Faith felt oddly comforted, then chastised herself for it.

Drake introduced his son. The little one responded by darting behind him.

When he peeked around Drake's back, Faith smiled. "Hi, William." She took half a step back to add distance between her and this cowboy who caused her to feel much too jittery and off-kilter.

Probably residual effects from the accident. That he'd caused... Something she'd do well to remember whenever he flashed that handsome smile in her direction. Men like him were all the same. They waltzed around in their boots and faded jeans, believing they were God's gift to women.

Drake introduced her, explaining why she was here and how they'd met.

"Wow." Elizabeth shook her head. "Way to make a lasting impression, big brother."

He hooked a thumb in his pocket and made a visual sweep of the area. "Where's Mom and Dad?"

A flicker of sadness flashed in the woman's eyes. With a nod, she pointed toward a picnic pavilion surrounded by tall oak trees. "Dad's already asking to go back home."

He cast Faith a sideways glance. "I'll go give him a holler, once I help this little lady load up on the grub."

"I'll take care of that." Elizabeth linked arms with Faith. "Come on. I'll introduce you to our pie ladies. The most important women to get to know in this town, especially since they've helped raise a chunk of the funding for Trinity Faith's restoration."

A chunk? Did that mean others had raised the rest, or that the committee had managed to come up with only part of the money? Otherwise this trip could set her back, after all her expenses, and she still didn't know if she could order replacement glass in time. She hadn't been able to get through to the supply store.

Weaving around adults and children, Elizabeth eventually led her to a pair of picnic tables. Faith fought to keep her overloaded plate of chicken, potato salad, green salad, Jell-O and two other salads she'd never heard of from toppling out of her hand.

Every few steps, Elizabeth stopped to introduce her to people—someone from the church finance committee, or a member of the fundraising team. The pastor's wife, mayor's daughter, town librarian.

Everyone had ideas on how the renovation should go and a story or three to go with them.

A hunchbacked woman with fluffy white hair placed a hand on Faith's forearm, nearly causing her to drop her lunch. "You know what we need? One of those crying rooms like them bigger churches got. And the paint in the foyer's too muted. We need something brighter. Like yellow."

"Margie, they can't just go around changing colors." A tall woman in a ruffled tank rolled her eyes.

Margie frowned. "Who says?"

"The cultural committee." The woman stepped closer, as if accepting a challenge. Or maybe initiating one. "Historical registry requirements and all."

When they reached the pavilion, Faith saw Drake squatting in front of an older man in a wheelchair. The man leaned back, arms crossed, his bushy eyebrows pinched in a scowl.

A silver-haired woman sat beside him. She watched Drake closely, while he seemed to be engaged in a tense conversation with the man.

"You should meet my parents." Elizabeth motioned toward the threesome. "My mom's declared herself the official town hostess. By the end of the week, she'll have you loaded up with casseroles, tomatoes and more coupons than you'll know what to do with."

"I, uh…sure."

Drake glanced up as they approached, his blue eyes latching on to Faith's and causing her cheeks to heat. He stood, feet shoulder distance apart, hand in his pocket. "Faith, this here's my dad,

Stanley Owens. He owns Owens Ranch out on Highway 59."

The man gave a brief nod, his tight expression softening some. "Welcome to Sage Creek."

Someone made a howling noise that sounded like a mix between Tarzan and a strangled pig.

Drake shook his head. "That troublemaker climbing that tree over there is my oldest, Trevor." He motioned to a child, also blond, swinging, then jumping from low-hanging branches. The kid looked to be about six or seven years old. "And this here's my mom, Sylvia." He placed his hand on the shoulder of the silver-haired woman. "Best baker this side of San Antone."

The woman waved her hand. "Don't know about that, but I do love to keep my family sufficiently sweetened." She winked at Drake, then motioned for Faith to sit on the picnic table bench beside her. "I hear you've been hired to help Drake, the town's most eligible bachelor, fix our church right up."

Heat flooded Faith's cheeks. Surely the woman wasn't implying…

His gaze met hers again, and her pulse skittered. She stiffened and looked away, then sat beside his mother and started forking bits of onion out of her green bean casserole.

"You've seen the place? Trinity Faith Church, I mean?" Sylvia asked. "Isn't that a fine how-do-you-do. God's hand if I ever saw it—Faith assigned, by faith, to restore Trinity Faith. I know there's an *amen* story to that one."

Faith blinked. "A what?"

"You know, how God brought you here to us."

"Well…" No sense telling this poor woman that God had absolutely nothing to do with her being here, or her choices, period. Faith had seen enough of the ugliness of religion growing up to know she wanted nothing to do with it.

"I've always loved history and art." She tucked a lock of hair behind her ear. "I have a subscription to *Lone Star Gems*." The most prestigious art and culture magazine in Texas, and the one she hoped would help salvage her career, so long as she managed to get a feature. "A few months ago, they did an article on some of Texas's oldest churches. They were all so beautiful and unique, I knew I had to see them. But while researching my trip, I read about your church's fire."

"So sad." Sylvia shook her head. "But I'm not worried none. You and Drake will fix that place up good as new." She flashed a grin.

Drake, the man who could spike her pulse with just a glance, working alongside her…

For two weeks, maybe longer…

Totally not a big deal, considering he wasn't her type. The man was country from his boots to his Stetson.

Still, she'd be wise to maintain an appropriate distance.

Chapter Three

Faith liked Drake's mom. She had stories for everything, many of them hilarious, and about half were about her son and grandkids. It was clear she cherished her role as Meemaw, as she was called.

As the afternoon wore on, Drake's boys started to bicker, his oldest teasing the little one by holding a Frisbee just out of reach. According to their father, the youngest was determined to be like his big brother, which often resulted in tears from the younger and taunting from the older. Little William ran after Trevor, then tripped on a branch and fell splat on his face. He remained there, crying and wailing.

"Oh!" Faith sprang to her feet, one hand on her mouth.

"Excuse me." Drake set his Coke on the picnic table and ambled to his son's side. Upon reaching him, Drake pulled him up, dropped to one knee and set the child on his other. "What's broken?"

William sniffed, tears streaking his dirty face.

"Your arm?" He lifted the boy's arm, wiggled it until he started to laugh. "Your leg?" He grabbed his son's leg, nearly causing him to topple over, if not for Drake's stabilizing arm on his back. "Oh, I know. Your ear." He stuck a finger in William's ear, causing him to squeal and squirm.

Faith laughed.

"Sure is good with those boys."

She turned to find one of the women among numerous Elizabeth had introduced Faith to—she couldn't remember her name—standing beside her, sucking on a chicken bone.

"Glad to see it." The woman leaned closer, hand cupped around her mouth. "I was worried, with his dad's accident and all. Thought Drake would go through another dark spell, like he did when his wife died. Didn't know who'd step in to take care of things then."

Drake was a widower? But he was so young, as were his kids. Faith felt her heart tug in his direction.

"Well." Drake's mom stood and began gathering used paper plates from the table. "I suppose it's getting to be that time."

His sister sprang to her feet. "Need help with Dad?"

"I…" She glanced at Drake.

As if sensing her attention, he tossed his son over his shoulder and hurried to them. "You and Dad ready to jet?" he asked his mother.

"I hate to put you out."

"Stop." His expression turned firm. He glanced about before catching Faith's eye. "Give me a minute?"

"Sure. No problem." The way Drake's father was scowling, his mom was wringing her hands and his sister was picking at her pinkie nail, Faith felt she'd stumbled into a private family squabble.

She helped with cleanup, trying to answer the seemingly endless questions random strangers fired her way.

One of the older women gave her a knowing smile and asked what she thought of the rancher's son.

As if she planned to stay for the duration.

She tossed her napkin into a nearby trash can. "I haven't." Regardless of how attractive she found Drake or how welcoming all these people were, she had no intention of living in a small town again.

Drake grabbed the handles of his dad's wheelchair. The terrain in front of them—grass dotted with bare patches and numerous dips, ridges and rises—made pushing the thing a challenge. Elizabeth must have suffered quite a workout to get Dad from the truck to the picnic table. Not to mention getting him into the truck in the first place.

They needed to figure something out. Soon. Tomorrow Drake would check on costs of wheel-chair lifts.

"Daddy, I help." His youngest ran to Drake's side.

Dad visibly tensed.

Because of William's request? Made sense. Dad had never been one to ask for help, never one to admit he needed it. Now he needed help with everything. With one quick statement, his three-year-old-grandson had called attention to this fact.

The man's entire life had shifted with one fall.

A fall that wouldn't have happened had Drake stayed to help on the ranch that day.

"How about you help Meemaw clean up," Drake said.

"But I strong." His tiny fingers gripped the smooth metal bars.

"I know you are." He gently pried the child's hands free. "Which is why Meemaw needs you." He glanced back to find Faith watching him, and a strange sensation heightened his senses.

Clearing his throat, he averted his gaze. Trevor, older by two and a half years, hung from a low-hanging branch about a hundred feet away. "Oh. Look what your brother's doing."

William's haloed head jerked in that direction, and his face lit up. In a flash, he was off, his chubby little arms pumping.

Drake chuckled. That boy was about as distractible as a puppy chasing a pack of baby chicks.

He headed toward his mom's SUV, offered one of the church members a passing nod and maneuvered his dad around a two-inch hole. "You get to talk to anyone?"

Dad hitched a shoulder up.

"I know Mom's glad you came. You need to get out more."

"Everyone knows what I need now?"

Ouch. "All's I'm saying is folks are glad to see you."

No response. These outings always put him in a mood. His doctor said to expect anger, and Drake got that. It had to smart something awful to lose the use of one's legs. But Dad wasn't the only one going through a major life change. He wasn't the only one mourning.

Drake looked at his mom, glad to see her surrounded by a group of ladies. He'd connect with her tomorrow to check how she was faring and what appointments Dad had this week that she might need help with.

He stopped as two barefoot boys ran in front of them, one of them clutching a football to his chest. "I have a feeling some of the church ladies will be bringing goodies to the work site tomorrow. I'll save you some."

Dad gave a slight nod. Better than a grunt.

"I was thinking of taking the boys fishing this weekend. Want to come?"

No response. *Lord, help me out here. How can I pull him out of this funk?*

When they reached his mom's SUV, one of Drake's buddies hurried to meet them. He waited for Drake to move Dad's footrests out of the way, then quietly stepped in. Mimicking Drake, he cupped a hand under Dad's left thigh, and with his other, gripped his forearm without a word. Asking would've only wounded Dad's pride.

Would it always be this way?

They lifted him in, then Drake secured his seat belt and shot him a smile. Receiving a frown in return, Drake closed the door with a suppressed sigh.

How did a person adapt to something like this? Especially a rancher who'd been handling bulls, mending fences and barns, and whatever else, for as long as Drake could remember? The man loved being outside. Loved doing.

Took pride in his role as protector and provider.

Drake rounded the vehicle to the driver's side to get the air-conditioning going. "Want the radio on while you wait for Mom?" He fiddled with the dial.

"Don't matter."

"All right then." He turned to Rural Radio so his dad could catch up on cattle prices—or would that stress him out? Remind him of the threat of losing the ranch? Drake flipped to the local country-and-western station and closed the door.

He released a heavy breath and scrubbed a hand over his face.

Bryce, one of his best friends since middle school, strolled over. "How're you holding up?"

He didn't answer right away. "We'll be all right."

"Christa is worried about your momma. Said she's hardly left the ranch since the accident."

"She's got to watch Dad." It was just like Bryce's wife to feel concerned, and likely a strong pull to help. That woman was one of the most caring people Drake knew.

"Figured as much. But…" He popped a few of his knuckles. "Maybe some of the Bible study gals could help out some. Take turns sitting with him."

Drake snorted. "That'll go over real well." He shot his dad a sideways glance.

"Yeah, well, it's not just about him, is it?" Bryce's gaze intensified.

Drake gave a quick nod and leaned back against the vehicle. "I'll talk to Mom and Elizabeth."

"Good enough. So…that girl, the one whose car you totaled—"

"I didn't total it."

"Pretty near. Not the smartest way to snag a woman, but I'm glad to know you're not completely blind."

"What're you talking about?"

"I see the way you look at her."

"I'm not interested in dating anyone, let alone a city girl. The boys have had enough to deal with."

"It's been three years. Your youngest doesn't even remember Lydia."

Drake winced and clenched his teeth to keep from snapping.

Bryce raised his hands, palms out. "Sorry. I didn't mean… That was stupid."

A tense silence stretched between them. "Regardless, she won't be here for long. And as far as I'm concerned she's not supposed to be here at all." Drake relayed all he knew about her, which wasn't much, and everything he remembered from the last church restoration planning meeting.

"I caught a look at the bids." Drake shoved a hand in his pocket. "Before the crew made their decision. She's an artist from some gallery. From what I could tell, she hasn't done more than a handful of stained glass restorations, if that."

"She can't be too inept. She got the contract, didn't she?"

"I'm not so sure."

"What do you mean?"

"I asked Mayor Pearson about it. Both of us remember the restoration team choosing Leaded Pane. He's going to go through all the bids tomorrow."

"So you're thinking that other outfit might show up in the morning, ready to get to work." His friend shook his head. "That'll be awkward."

"Tell me about it." As if Drake didn't have enough drama to deal with. Then again, that was the best-case scenario. The worst would be her actually doing the job and proving incompetent. "The restoration team'll handle it. Let her down gently and send her on her way."

He glanced at his dad. He had to be getting cranky, sitting in the SUV like he was.

Drake turned to see what was keeping his mom, then froze.

Faith stood a few feet away, and based on her expression, had been there for some time. Long enough to hear most everything.

"Hello." Her tone was clipped.

Bryce cleared his throat and took a half step back, as if distancing himself from the mess Drake had just created.

"Hey." Drake swallowed.

While he fidgeted, trying to untangle his tongue, Bryce tipped his hat to Drake's mom and sister as they approached. "Mrs. Owens. Elizabeth."

"Such a lovely evening." His mom smiled,

completely oblivious to the tension filling the air. "Where's that beautiful wife and son of yours? I wanted to say hi, but, well…"

She'd never left Dad's side except to fill plates. Bryce was right. She needed a break. He and Elizabeth would have to figure out how to make that happen. Regularly.

"They're probably still down by the lake trying to catch snakes," Bryce said. "Or I should say, Elijah's chasing snakes while his momma's standing on the tallest rock, praying this phase of his passes quickly."

"Good luck with that one." His mom laughed. "Well, I suppose we should go. You ready, Elizabeth?"

"Yes, ma'am." She flicked everyone a wave, then turned to Faith. "We'll see you Friday?"

Drake raised his eyebrows. When had Faith and his sister gotten so chummy? And what did she mean by *we*? Not that it mattered. The woman would be heading back to Austin soon enough.

Except she was going nowhere right now. Her car was in the shop. Because of him.

Faith pressed her tongue to the roof of her mouth to keep from saying something stupid, and accompanied Drake to the truck. So he didn't want her here. Thought she couldn't do the job. The cocky, small-minded… She'd just have to prove him—and everyone else in Sage Creek—wrong.

Like she'd been trying to do with her dad for the past decade, ever since she dropped out of college to pursue a career in art. That had gone over real well; the professor's daughter hadn't made it through her junior year.

And if Drake was right, if somehow she was here by mistake? She'd be out a good deal of money. And who knew how long it would take the town mechanic to fix her vehicle?

Which Mr. Cowboy had totaled. She should make him pay for her hotel. If the restoration team gave her the boot, that's exactly what she'd do. She had no choice. She didn't have the money for a random, unexpected "vacation."

How was she supposed to get to the church and back to her hotel each day?

Eyeing Drake, she frowned. She had no intention of becoming dependent on some macho cowboy.

No matter how handsome.

Grabbing on to the handle above the door, she hoisted herself into the sauna-like truck, her long skirt twisting around her legs. With a grimace, she fought to free herself from the fabric as gracefully as possible.

He engaged the engine, and hot air pelted Faith's face. "Whew." He angled the vents away from both of them, then shifted into Reverse.

"Far's I can tell, Mr. Johnson left an hour or so ago. He should be back at the hotel now."

Rocks clanged against the truck's undercarriage as he turned onto the dirt road leading back to town. "I'll give him a call to make sure." He pulled his phone from his back pocket, put it on speaker, then set it on the dash. "I lost my Bluetooth."

It rang four times before anyone answered. "Hey-lo. Cedar View Inn. Where the coffee's hot, the cable's connected and the view's pristine."

"Hey, Mr. Johnson. It's me, Drake."

"Figured as much. You calling about that gal friend of yours?"

"Yes, sir. We're heading your way, if that's all right."

"Course it is. I'll go turn the air on in her room now."

"She'd be mighty obliged, I'm sure." Call over, he set his phone in his cup holder and turned onto the paved street. "What'd you think of the picnic?"

"It was nice. The food was good."

He nodded and drummed his fingers on the steering wheel. "You and my sister seemed to hit it off."

She gave a one-shoulder shrug. "She and your mom want to learn how to paint." She gave a soft laugh. "They said they'd trade me a home-cooked meal for lessons." It felt awkward saying that. It would probably feel awkward going, but…those dinners could save her a chunk of change. Money she'd desperately need, especially if she found herself stuck here, unemployed, with hotel fees to pay.

This would be a first, to get fired before even getting started.

And if Mr. Cowboy's insurance didn't come through and he decided not to honor his word, she'd be in the red.

Her phone rang. She glanced at the screen and exhaled. It was R & T Glass Supply. "Hello?"

"Faith. Sorry I missed your call."

"No problem. Listen, I'm sort of in a bind here." She explained her predicament and pulled a pocket notebook from her purse. On it, she'd written all the details needed to make her order. "You wouldn't happen to have any more cobalt-blue and jade-green sheets on hand, would you?" She read the item number for each.

"Nope. But I can get some in."

She rubbed her temple, pushing back an emerging headache. "You want to check? I'll hold."

"Don't need to. I remember your order. Didn't see the need to buy any extra."

Great. It could take weeks to get those sheets in, time she didn't have. "Any chance you can rush order some?"

"Sure, but it'll be expensive."

"How much are we talking?"

"You'd need to pay the freight fee. Five hundred bucks."

She winced and shot Drake a glance, to find him watching her. Probably waiting to calculate how big of a check he'd need to write, considering this was all his fault. What kind of man drove sixty miles per hour on a wobbly tire?

"How soon could you get them in?"

"Don't know. Forty-eight hours. Maybe sooner."

"Great. Let's do it." She shifted the phone from her mouth. "I sure hope your insurance comes through on this."

Drake pulled into the hotel between her trailer and a beat-up, pale blue pickup. "If they don't, I'll reimburse you personally."

She studied him. Yet another promise from a man she knew nothing about. Except that he was an irresponsible driver who liked to take risks on the open highway. Only this time, she didn't have any witnesses to hold him accountable.

"You'll sign on it?"

He frowned, but then his expression softened and one side of his mouth quirked up. "Sure. No problem."

She wrote out a simple agreement, then handed over the paper and her pen.

He signed, then returned it.

"Thanks." She grabbed her purse, ready to bolt.

"I'll pick you up at eight tomorrow morning."

To take her to a job he felt certain she couldn't do.

She had every intention of proving him wrong.

Chapter Four

At seven the next morning, Faith stood in front of a small, tarnished mirror, giving her hair more attention than she had in all her teen years combined. It didn't help that she'd woken to find three zits on her face, one smack in the center of her forehead. Nor that she was about to start a job where she was clearly unwanted.

The fact that she cared irked her considerably. This wasn't Alpine, nor was she a lanky, awkward nerd—the kid that never fit in and everyone else made fun of—anymore.

Instead, she was an insecure, nearly impoverished adult who, according to her father, wasted her time chasing fanciful dreams.

She grabbed her eyebrow brush with a huff. If Mr. Cowboy and his friends planned to send her packing this morning, at least she'd look good when they did. She had just finished penciling in her brows when a thought hit. She'd forgotten to change her shipping info, which meant they'd send her glass supplies to the store in Austin, and not to Sage Creek.

Was it too late to adjust her order?

R & T's wouldn't be open for another two and a half hours. By then, her supplies could be halfway to Austin.

She paced her tiny hotel room. With her car in the shop and no access to public transportation, how was she supposed to pick up the glass?

Drake could drive her. The man who believed she was an incompetent artist and who was just waiting for the restoration committee to give her the boot. Her empty stomach tensed.

Regardless, he was the only logical solution, and all things considered, it was the least he could do. She shot him a text: I need a ride to Austin to pick up my glass when it comes in.

She tucked her phone into her purse, gathered up some historical photographs and headed to the hotel lobby in search of breakfast.

The small, wood-paneled room, empty except for two men occupying separate tables, smelled like burned coffee and Pine-Sol. How did this place stay open? The bigger question was how did a town this small have the revenue to pay for a major church restoration?

That might not be her concern much longer.

The more she thought about Drake, him picking her up, taking her to Austin, the more jittery she felt. Scrolling through her Facebook, she tried to distract herself with photos of kittens.

"Looks like your ride's here." Mr. Johnson hooked his thumb toward the parking lot, then grabbed a pink-frosted doughnut from the food counter.

She gathered her things and stepped outside, her heart stuttering when Drake's eyes met hers. She dropped her gaze, set her stuff on the passenger seat, then faced her trailer.

She needed it at the job site but was in no mood to ask Mr. Cocky Cowboy for help, even if he owed it to her.

"Need a hand?"

His citrusy, earthy cologne invaded her senses and stole her words.

His mouth quirked up in a lopsided grin that made her cheeks flame. "Rig's unlocked." He jerked his head toward the truck, then began hitching her trailer to it.

With a brisk nod she hoped conveyed confidence, she climbed into the cab to wait. Cool air circulated throughout the interior, his aftershave merging with the scents of wood chips, leather and stale coffee.

Less than five minutes later, they were backing out of the parking lot and heading toward the work site.

"I got your text." He adjusted his visor to block rays from the rising sun.

She gave a curt nod.

"When were you thinking?"

"Whenever the glass comes in. Hopefully by tomorrow afternoon."

A tendon twitched in his jaw. "Austin, right?"

"Yeah. Just north of downtown."

He massaged the back of his neck. "That'll be tough, with the restoration and all."

She crossed her arms. "That's not my fault, now, is it?"

His eyebrows shot up. He glanced at the rear-view mirror, then back to the road. "Reckon you're right. I'll make it work. Just let me know when."

"Thanks."

An uncomfortable silence stretched between them.

"How'd you sleep?" He slid her a sideways glance. "You like the place all right?"

"It was nice. Quiet."

"Most everything in Sage Creek is."

Was it? Or was it a town filled with gossipy chatter about how she wasn't supposed to be here? She'd likely find out soon enough.

In an effort to relax before the tension in her shoulders turned to knots, she gazed out her side window, watching the tall, golden grass wave and shimmy in the morning breeze.

They reached the end of downtown, if you could call it that, and Drake took a sharp left.

They continued through a residential area with single-story brick homes shaded by mature trees. Half the yards boasted American flags, while rusted or wooden wagon wheels decorated a handful of others.

The neighborhood dead-ended with an expanse of trees in front of them and a gravel road veering to their right. Drake turned onto it, dust seeping through the vents and tickling Faith's nose.

She sneezed.

"Bless you."

His smiling eyes sent an unwelcomed tingle through her. "Thank you."

Straightening, she looked away, determined to keep her rebellious hormones, or whatever kept snagging on the man's appealing grin, in check. She had no intention of falling for Mr. Cowboy, or staying in Sage Creek any longer than necessary.

He parked, and she took in a deep breath, hoping the beauty of the historic church before her, with its gothic windows and steeply pitched roof, would soothe her nerves. If only she could recapture the peace and joy she'd felt when she came out to do the estimate—when no one else had been on the property except for Lucy Carr, from the cultural committee.

This morning, cars filled the small gravel parking lot and at least half a dozen men and women, some in jeans and T-shirts, others in business casual, dotted the church lawn.

She touched the door handle, reluctant to leave the vehicle. "Um… What's this about?"

"I 'spect folks coming to help."

Hopefully, with the construction end of things, because she had no intention of letting anyone mess with the church's fragile antique windows. Anticipation surfaced at the thought of touching glass from an era that in many towns had been lost and forgotten.

Though she'd taken a plethora of photos during her estimate, she itched to take more. They would provide months' worth of inspiration later. Jewelry that captured the multicolored rays of sunlight as it dispersed through the dusty sanctuary. Glass mosaics with the same sharp, dramatic elements displayed in the castle-like bell tower.

But first, she needed to focus on the task at hand…assuming they still wanted her.

She gathered her things and stepped out into the muggy, morning air.

"Ah, Drake, there you are." A plump elderly woman with wiry gray hair poofing out from beneath a yellow bandanna shuffled toward them. "I was starting to think you'd never get here." One of her knee-highs sagged halfway down her shin.

"Ma'am." He greeted her with a tip of his Stetson. "It's just after eight."

"My point exactly. Some of these folks have been here for going on thirty minutes already. They've been patient enough, but I worried, any longer and they'd start meddling where they didn't belong. You know how folks can be."

His mouth twitched as if suppressing a chuckle. "That I do."

"Oh, I made you breakfast." She slipped a massive green purse-like contraption off her shoulder, snapped it open and produced a mound of something wrapped in a paper towel. Then, as if seeing Faith for the first time, she said, "Oh, hello. You must be Faith Nichols."

"Yes, ma'am."

"I've been wanting to meet with you." She rummaged through her purse, unloading numerous random items onto the grass. Paper clips, pieces of gum, half a candy bar, what looked to be an old hair roller. "I printed a bunch of pictures, designs, whatnot, off the internet. Although some are black-and-white, they should give you an idea as to…" She huffed. "Now where did those pages go?" She leveled her gaze on Faith. "Library charges five cents a copy. Can you imagine?" She resumed her search until a small mound lay at her feet.

Finally, she threw her hands up with a loud exhalation. "Wouldn't you know it? I bet I left those papers on my kitchen table. I got distracted when my pill alarm went off, fought to get my orange juice open…"

The woman continued retelling every moment of her morning.

Faith exchanged a glance with Drake. His eyes were dancing with suppressed laughter, giving him a boyish appearance she found much too appealing.

She cleared her throat. "If you'll excuse—"

"Drake, Faith, good to see you."

She turned to see Lucy Carr, the president of the cultural committee, striding toward them, clipboard in one hand and what looked to be file folders in the other.

Drake laid a hand on the arm of the woman with the green purse. "Can I catch up with you later?"

The woman waved a hand. "Of course. You know where to find me." And then she shuffled away.

Faith offered Lucy her most professional smile. "Ma'am."

"You both ready to work your magic?" Lucy shaded her eyes and gazed toward the fire-damaged church. "To turn this place from a mess of ashes to beauty?" She laughed. "Get it? Ashes to beauty?"

Faith frowned. "Um, not exactly."

"It's from the Bible—"

"Listen." Drake scratched his jaw. "Think I can speak with you a minute? In private, I mean?"

"Ah…" Lucy glanced from Drake to her clipboard, then back again. "Sure. Soon as we finish—"

"Actually, I think now might be best."

A hollow sensation filled Faith's gut as she looked from one to the other. He wasn't seriously going to try to get her fired, was he? The guarded look on Drake's face suggested she wasn't going to like the answer.

Chapter Five

The vulnerability in Faith's eyes, almost like she was begging not to be rejected, tugged at Drake's heart.

He felt bad for wanting her off the project.

But it wasn't personal. This was a big restoration, in terms of money and sentimental value. To the folks of Sage Creek, Trinity Faith was much more than a church. It preserved memories going back since the town was first founded. Countless baptisms and weddings had been held here.

It was where Drake and his wife had fallen in love and, years later, where they'd said their vows. And where her funeral had been held, the whole town coming out to pay their respects. Though he'd worked through his grief, he still wanted to hold tight to his memory of that day.

Besides, he couldn't let his mom down. She'd been crushed once she'd seen the destruction left by the fire. Then came Dad's accident. Drake couldn't do anything about the latter, but he could make sure the church got repaired, to as good or even better a condition than it had been in before. Even if that meant hurting Ms. City Girl's feelings.

Faith took a visible breath. "Where's the restroom?"

"Inside, all the way to the back, turn right." Lucy pointed to the church, then faced Drake as Faith headed off. "What's up? Everything okay with your daddy?"

"Far's I know. He was sleeping when I dropped the kids off this morning."

"And your mom? She's holding up okay?"

"A mite tired, but yeah."

The woman released a gust of air. "I'm glad. I worried you were going to tell me you can't go through with this job. I know the timing stinks, with your dad's accident and all. Everything's good, then?"

"Not exactly." He guided her toward an old picnic table near the back of the church.

"All right, then. What's wrong?"

"Did Mayor Pearson talk with you? About Leaded Pane?" He'd thought about having this conversation with Lucy yesterday at the picnic, but she'd left before he'd had a chance. When he tried calling that evening, her phone hadn't let him leave a message, saying her inbox was full.

"The bids." Lucy smoothed her long skirt and sat. "He told you about that, then?"

"No. I saw them for myself, when y'all were making your decisions. So that I could plan out my end, remember?"

"Right." She rubbed her forehead. "Everything's gotten jumbled, I'll give you that. But I don't see what we can do at this point."

"Tell Faith something must have been miscommunicated somewhere, that you're sorry, but… What time did Leaded Pane say they'd show up?"

"They aren't coming."

"What do you mean? Why?"

"Because we never called them. We got the bids mixed up. For now, all's I can tell you is Jenna Anne told Faith she got the job."

"What do you mean?"

"What I'm saying is—"

"What she's saying is you're stuck with me."

At least now she knew they weren't going to give her the boot. Not unless Mr. Cowboy made a stink. Though he looked ready to crawl under that lopsided picnic table he was sitting at.

"Faith." Lucy sprang to her feet. "I didn't see you there."

She leveled her gaze on Drake. "So I gathered." *Easy, girl. Don't get yourself fired.* She faced Lucy. "You wanted to speak with me?"

The woman stared at her. "I... Uh... I wanted to make sure you have everything you need to get started."

"I do."

"If you have any questions or run into any difficulties, you've got my number."

"I do."

Lucy gave a quick nod, looked from Faith to Drake then back to Faith, and then walked away.

Faith intended to do the same. "If you'll excuse me, I have work to do." She spun on her heel and marched, head held high, toward her trailer.

Drake jogged after her. He caught up and matched her step for step. "Need help unloading?"

She stopped and glared at him. "Contrary to what you might think, Mr.—"

"Call me Drake."

Oh, she could think of half a dozen other things she'd like to call him. "—I'm not completely inept, Drake." Reaching her trailer out of breath, she dug through her pocket for the key to the dead-bolted doors. She suppressed a moan. Of course it was in her purse, which, in her nervousness, she'd left in Drake's truck.

He stepped into her peripheral vision. "Everything all right?"

"Absolutely. Is your truck locked?"

"Nope. Why? You need something?"

"I do." She strode toward his vehicle, still attached to her trailer, with as much self-respect as she could muster. She knew better than to let someone like Drake get to her. Every town had men like him, cowboys who sweet-talked naive and gullible women, swept them off their feet, then left them heartbroken.

Like Josh had done to her.

Those type of men weren't worth a second thought, except she did have to work with Drake. Joy. She yanked open his passenger side door and grabbed her purse.

A moment later, she returned to find him standing in the same place, watching her.

Ignoring his steady gaze, she fumbled with her lock. Then, hands slick from the mounting Texas humidity, she strained to unload sheets of glass from her trailer.

"I cleared out the back shed for you—so you could have uninterrupted workspace." He motioned toward a small, dilapidated building past the far corner of the church. Thick, overgrown trees and bushes pressed up against it on either side. In front of it sat what appeared to be numerous metal tubs.

"Does the shed have electricity?"

"Yep. The sanctuary's going to be a mess, with us tearing up the carpet and all." He eyed the various colored sheets spread out beside her. "Hold on. I'll drive your trailer closer to your work area. So we don't need to carry everything so far."

"Fine." She stepped back to give him room to maneuver his rig then followed him on foot to the shed.

He parked and stepped out. "I'll unload those sheets for you."

"No." Her tone came out clipped. She took a deep breath. "I appreciate your help, but these are expensive and very fragile."

"It's not like I'm going to juggle the things."

Ignoring him, she climbed inside the trailer to get to her glass cutting tools. He offered to help a couple more times, and she declined, rather firmly and probably with much less professionalism than appropriate.

She nearly ate her words when she got to her portable grinder. The cord had gotten stuck beneath the box of lead came used to join cut glass pieces together.

So she'd take that out, too.

Ten minutes later, sweat trickling down her temples and static electricity frizzing her hair, she stood surrounded by nearly all her supplies.

Drake eyed the items. "You always make things so hard on yourself?"

"Excuse me?"

"You make a habit of digging your heels in like this?"

She fisted her hands and scowled. The nerve of that man!

He leaned over to pick up a blue sheet of glass.

She nearly lurched at him. "What're you doing?"

"Carrying this into the shed, because even though I'm tempted to let you keep on fighting with all this on your own, we've got a project to complete. And at the rate you're going, the church windows won't be finished before Christmas."

She stared after him, mouth agape, as he marched across the patchy lawn, nodding to folks as he went.

Fine. If he wanted to do the heavy lifting, so be it. "Be careful with those. Make sure to place them in a safe spot."

Shaking his head, he disappeared inside the heavily shadowed shed.

With a huff, she followed, hefting her box of window-cleaning supplies. She stood in the doorway, watching as he carefully set her glass against a plywood wall. An old, deformed rake, a metal gas can and other tools lined the opposite wall, and light emanated from a single bulb centered in the ceiling.

Ugh. So she'd cut her pieces outside.

"I had my ranching buddies bring these." He motioned toward the rusted metal tubs, which she now recognized as feeding troughs. "Will this be enough, you think?"

"For…?"

"To soak your glass in, get all the dust and

grime and whatnot off them. Isn't that how you do it?"

Duh. She knew she'd forget something, as if she hadn't looked unprofessional before. But feeding troughs? "I hadn't thought to use farm equipment."

He gave a slight shrug. "When Leaded Pane came out a few years ago, they brought a tub, but that was when only one window needed cleaning. I figured there might be more to tackle."

She nodded. For uniformity, she'd need to wash them all. "I appreciate the forethought."

"No problem. Need anything else?"

"I'm good."

"Hey, boss?" She saw a potbellied man in coveralls waving Drake over.

"Excuse me." He tipped his hat to her, then sauntered off.

She gazed up at the side windows of the church, each at a height that made her stomach knot.

Lucy had assured her, when Faith made her bid, that she could use the scaffolding they already had on hand, but that probably belonged to Drake and his crew. The thought of asking to borrow it, even though technically it was considered on-site equipment, made her jaw clench.

The man obviously didn't like outsiders and clearly thought she was the worst person for this job, probably because she was a woman.

She'd just have to show him and his committee friends how wrong they were.

Half an hour later, with notes, measurements and photographs in hand, she circled the property. When she reached the other side of the church, she practically cheered. There, two older men stood a few feet from the back of a dented white van, assembling scaffolding.

"Howdy." The taller of the two touched the brim of a sweat-stained ball cap.

"Hi." Hopefully these guys held women in higher esteem than Drake did. She approached with an extended hand and introduced herself. "I'm here to work on the windows."

Both men faced her with feet shoulder width apart.

The one on the right mopped his brow with a gray rag. "So I heard."

What did that mean? Drake had probably been flapping his mouth to everyone out here. She resisted the urge to ask, and maintained a forced smile. "If it's not too much of a bother, when you're done assembling this—" she indicated the rolling aluminum tower they'd been building "—would you mind if I borrowed it? Briefly."

They exchanged glances, and the shorter of the two tugged on the skin beneath his chin. "Mind if I ask what for?"

Drake joined them. "Everything okay here?"

"Perfectly." She faced him and repeated her request.

He studied her a moment, his deep gaze latching on to hers, then he pivoted to look at the windows on this side of the building. "You need us to get the broken panes down for you?"

"It'd be best if I did that."

"Woman, if you think I'm going to let you—"

"Let me?" What century had this man stepped out of? "Why, sir—" She donned a demure voice, placed a hand under her chin and batted her eyes. "—we women can do all sorts of difficult things. We can write our numbers, read books, and not just the ones with pretty pictures."

The gentleman in the ball cap snickered, then covered with a cough.

Drake's mouth flattened. "Fellas, can you give us a minute?"

"No problem."

His friends sauntered off, and Drake faced her. "Look, I think we got off on the wrong foot here. But if we're going to be working together, we need to find a way to get along."

She released a breath, her tense shoulders going slack. She hated to admit it, but he was right. And she was better than this. So the man was infuriating and chauvinistic.

And handsome enough to land on the cover of an outdoorsman magazine.

"I agree." She readjusted her ponytail. "But I can't allow you or anyone else to remove those windows. The glass is much too fragile."

"I see." He scratched his jaw. "How about we work together, and you show me how?"

She wanted to protest, but at that height, and with the weight of those leaded panes, she'd need extra hands.

"Fine. But it's imperative you follow my directions precisely." Before he could respond, she spun around and marched back to her trailer for duct tape.

She returned to find him right where she'd left him—awaiting further instruction. A slight smile tugged her mouth. "Did you want to help me wheel the scaffolding against the siding?"

His gaze bounced from her to the unbroken window. "I'm not trying to tell you how to do your job or nothing, but that window looks just fine to me."

"That's why they hired me to restore the stained glass and you to remove bat guano." According to Lucy, the summer before, they'd discovered the church had a bad infestation in the attic. Apparently they'd managed to get all the critters out a while ago, and prevent them from entering. But they hadn't, as of yet, cleaned up the mess.

Though Drake probably had his crew taking care of that, while he did more important things.

Red blotches climbed up his neck. But, mouth set in a firm line, he complied.

Faith wasn't exactly making friends. She needed to start playing nice, before she dug herself into a mess that not only cost her this job, but tarnished her professional reputation, as well.

Chapter Six

The next morning, Faith rode her bike down sleepy Main Street on the way to work and breathed in the yeasty cinnamon smells. The aroma, tinged with a hint of coffee, drifted from a tall, narrow building on the corner with shake siding, a steep roof and forest-green trim.

A sign dangled from cast-iron chains above the door, The Literary Sweet Spot etched into the maroon wood. Various books, some new and others well-loved, decorated the rectangular windows flanking the entrance. Two women in running gear sat nursing coffees at one of three outside tables.

Faith needed to stop in one of these evenings, relax with a caramel latte.

She turned onto B Street and passed a handful of single-story homes with chain-link fences and cheery flowerbeds on her way to the dirt road leading to the church. Though it wasn't yet

8:00 a.m., Drake was already there, and apparently had gotten his truck back. If only the mechanic finished the repairs on hers as quickly.

Drake stood talking to a tall, lanky man dressed in white coveralls. A wheelbarrow waited a few feet away.

Faith slowed to a stop and unsnapped her helmet. She leaned her bike against her trailer, fluffed her mashed hair and approached. "Morning."

"Howdy." Drake touched the brim of his hat, a slight smile crinkling the skin around his blue eyes. The man was handsome enough to make a girl's knees knock together. Too bad he was such a jerk.

Then again, she hadn't exactly been a spoonful of sugar.

"Gonna be a hot one today." He hooked a thumb through his belt loop. "Might top one hundred."

His crewman let out a long, low whistle. "That attic will feel like a sauna. You sure you want to help?"

"I'm not above getting my hands dirty."

"Some things don't change." He clamped a hand on Drake's shoulder and grinned at Faith. "This fella never asks his guys to do something he himself won't."

She raised an eyebrow. Impressive. Maybe he wasn't as cocky as she'd thought. Though he still had an issue with females on scaffolding. Speaking of which…

"Listen, I need to get the rest of the windows down today, so I can start soaking them."

"No problem." Drake turned to his friend. "You go ahead and get started. I'll meet you up there in a bit."

The guy nodded and sauntered away.

"Back side?"

"Yep." She followed him to the church. Waited while he grabbed the scaffolding from where one of his men had been peeling away soggy drywall the day before. Then she helped him guide the contraption over crevices and clumps of overgrown grass to the first of three arching windows in back.

"You hear about your car yet?" he asked.

"It should be done today or tomorrow." She raised crossed fingers.

"Good news. Any problems working with my insurance company?"

"Not in the least."

"Glad to hear it. I was worried. I mean, I know what my policy says and all, but well, you know." He held the scaffolding steady, apparently ready for her to ascend it.

Classic alpha protector, only for some reason, this morning that didn't irk her like it might have the day before. She wasn't sure that was a good thing, considering the way her pulse kicked up a notch whenever his gaze snagged hers.

"Unfortunately, I do." She slipped her roll of tape onto her wrist to free her hands. "I've experienced how difficult it can be to get insurance companies to pay out." She started to climb. "This was my third accident in as many years, and all equally bizarre."

"Really?" He followed her up the scaffolding.

"First, a turkey came flying toward my windshield." She started taping the pieces to stabilize them.

"Dinner."

"What?"

"You know, the turkey. Roadkill grub." He gave a mischievous smile.

"Funny. Luckily, the bird swooped out of the way just in time. Unfortunately, I'd already slammed on my brakes, resulting in a pileup that completely totaled my car. The insurance companies battled it out for months to determine who was at fault."

She tore off a long section of duct tape with her teeth, then tossed the roll to him so he could do the same. "Then, one night, it was raining pretty hard. The roads were slick, and my windshield wipers were making the most annoying screech."

"So you were distracted."

"Maybe. Next thing I know, there's this shiny

ball in the middle of the road. Only it wasn't a ball. It was an armadillo."

He winced. "Maybe you better ditch the car and keep the bike."

"At the very least, I need to—" Her phone rang, and she pulled it from her back pocket. Finally! R & T Glass Supply. Hopefully, with good news.

"This is Faith."

"Hey, girl." It was Thomas, the owner. "Your order came in."

"Awesome. I'm on my way. I'm about two hours out."

"I'll be here."

She slid her phone back into her pocket and faced Drake. "You ready for a road trip?"

"Uh…" He blinked and made a visual sweep of the property. "I've got the insulation folks coming in a bit. Need to ask them some questions."

"When are they supposed to arrive?"

"Not sure. Before lunch. Plus, I need to watch my boys while my sister gets her hair done."

"Your kids okay with car rides? I really need my glass. Like yesterday."

He scratched his jaw, where a muscle twitched periodically. "Sure. No problem. Just let me tell my crew what's going on."

Thirty minutes later, they were in his truck heading north on I-35, his boys strapped in behind them. Some audio story played through the speakers, about a rat and a cat who became friends.

After about ten minutes, his youngest started squirming. "I want out, Daddy." He kicked the back of Faith's seat four times in rapid succession.

"Stop that." Drake reached around and grabbed William's ankle.

"It's no big deal." Faith turned around and offered the little one a smile, trying to think of some way to entertain him. She had been a bit demanding. Though she felt bad for the boys, Drake had put her in a bind. He'd taken a calculated risk the minute he drove on wobbly wheels. Unless they'd been fine before and hadn't come loose until he'd picked up speed. Still, the accident was his fault, and she needed to get to Austin.

"This Mike, the guy who's working on my car. He's not the one who replaced your tires, is he?"

Drake slid a glance her way. "Yep."

Lovely. No telling what shape her vehicle would be in by the time she got it back.

Drake adjusted his air-conditioning vent. "He's the best mechanic in the county."

Was that supposed to make her feel better?

"Everyone makes a mistake." Drake switched lanes to pass a slow-moving Chevy. "Though in Mike's defense, the day I took my truck to get new tires, I got a call from my mom with an emergency at the ranch I needed to manage. So, I was kind of in a hurry and rushed Mike a bit."

William started to fuss again. Faith pulled a sketchbook and drawing supplies from her bag, and rotated toward the boys. "You like to draw?"

William's pudgy-cheeked frown slowly smoothed out, though his bottom lip remained protruded.

"I do!" Trevor, Drake's oldest, sat forward and reached out his hand.

"Yes, ma'am?" Drake caught his son's eye in the rearview mirror.

"Yes, ma'am. I do, please."

The excitement in his eyes warmed her heart and reminded her of her first art class. She must've been seven or eight, back when she didn't know a flat brush from a filbert. But something about the colors, the time to create, and Mrs. Sack, her teacher, had made her come alive.

"What color do you want?" She held out her pencils.

"Blue. No, green. Brown. I mean… Can I have red?"

"Me, too! Me, too!" William tugged on the back of her seat.

Faith laughed. "Just so happens I have two reds." Technically, one crimson and the other rose. She handed them over, and felt her face flush when Drake cast her an admiring glance.

"Thanks," he said.

"Well, I figure their boredom's my fault, so…"

"Can you help me?" Trevor's little hand clutching his wrinkled paper appeared in her peripheral vision.

"Sure." She took the page. "What would you like me to draw?"

"A cow. And a horse. With a barn and tall yellow flowers that always fall over."

She looked at Drake with a raised eyebrow.

"Sunflowers."

"Ah. I can do that." She started to sketch.

"That drawing there's not too shabby," Drake said a few moments later, glancing at it briefly before gazing back at the highway.

She kept her eyes on the paper, suddenly feeling like a teenager on her first date. "Thanks."

"I remember you said you're an artist. What all do you do?"

"A little of everything." She began shading a monitor barn with a raised center roof. "Oil paintings, acrylics. Jewelry, mosaics and stained glass lampshades."

"Nice. I'm about as creative as a doorknob."

The admiration in his voice sent a flutter through her midsection. She cleared her throat, feeling a need for casual conversation when her phone pinged with an incoming email. She opened it and snorted. "Oh, my."

"Care to share?"

"Someone gave my contact information to that little old lady from the church—the one who printed off all those images."

"Mrs. Doris Harper?"

"She just flooded my inbox with about a dozen—" Her phone pinged again. "—or more photographs."

"Helpful."

The boys started singing some song about toads and armadillos.

"Oh, she's been 'helping' me at the church quite a bit. This morning, she brought over home-made cleaning supplies. They smelled like vinegar, peppermint and something else I couldn't place. It about made my lip curl."

His deep, throaty laugh chipped at her defenses. "She means well. But living by herself like she does, I guess she has all the time and freedom to give her quirks free rein."

"How long has she been at the clergy house near the church?"

"Going on ten years, plus or minus. She's sort of taken ownership of the place."

"So I discovered."

"Gives her something to feel proud of. A purpose. For years, she stayed with her sister. They were schoolteachers—never married. Her sister died about fifteen years ago, and not long after, Mrs. Harper started acting funny. Like she wasn't all there half the time."

As the road curved, he moved his visor to the side window. "Folks got worried. The church decided it'd be best to keep her close, so they asked her to move in to the parish house to help mind the place."

"That was nice of them."

"We take care of our own here in Sage Creek."

Her heart pricked as a memory surfaced. She was maybe eleven years old, and her mom had brought her to the one-room country church just outside of Alpine. It was midafternoon, and the place was nearly empty. Mom had gone to talk with the pastor, a bald-headed old man who always smelled like tacos.

Mom had handed her some paper and markers and shooed her away, but Faith had lingered close by. She hadn't caught much, except the pastor telling Mom to "lean on her sisters in Christ," using the exact phrase Drake used about taking care of our own.

Her parents had divorced less than a year later.

"Daddy, I got to go potty!"

"Me, too! Me, too!"

Shaking his head, he merged off the freeway. "Seems the boys and I got business to take care of."

Faith's phone rang. She glanced at the screen

and smiled. It was Toni, her closest friend and most faithful cheerleader.

She answered. "Hey, Toni. What's up?"

"A lot. Good stuff, girl. Like potential career-saving stuff."

"Sounds interesting." She resisted becoming too hopeful. Toni was known for her crazy, impossible-to-implement ideas.

Drake pulled up to a box-like convenience store and gas station, jumped out and began corralling the boys.

"It is." Toni paused. "Do I hear kids in the background?"

Holding a child by each hand, Drake strolled to the entrance, then stopped to open the door for a pregnant lady walking out.

The man was straight out of a country song, where muscular, boot-wearing men danced the two-step, corralled cattle and swept naive and unsuspecting women off their feet.

But Drake seemed legit. He got along with his parents, treated quirky old ladies with kindness and respect, was a devoted father...

He'd probably been a great husband, too. Not that Faith had any business thinking that way.

Besides, he was country through and through, and she had no intention of dating another cowboy.

Her last smooth-talking, Stetson-wearing boyfriend had left her for a curvy, flirty, party-going blonde.

"Yoo-hoo. Earth to Faith."

"Sorry." *Got distracted by a handsome cowboy with two adorable kids.* "Can you repeat that?"

"I was telling you about my solution to your problem. One would think you'd be more interested."

"What do you got?"

"What would you say if I told you I got you into a private showing at the Honey Locust?"

"You serious? *The* Honey Locust? The one in the Domain?"

"Yep."

That gallery displayed work from some of the world's top artists. "Why would they want my stuff?"

"Don't sell yourself short, girlie. I've always said you were talented."

"Maybe, but I'm also a nobody."

"A local nobody. They're partnering with the city for one of those highlighting-the-locals events. Plus, I got connections."

"Wow. Okay. When?"

"In two weeks. They want all the pieces to have some sort of Texas theme."

"Oh." The air deflated from her lungs. That meant she'd have to make something new, which she didn't have time for. But this was too great an opportunity to blow. "If I do that, make something Texan, I mean, they'll for sure take it?"

"Not exactly."

"Of course." Always a few tweaks shy of for sure. Story of her life.

"But the odds are good. I got pull, my friend. This could be huge. Media, rubbing elbows with Austin's elite—the art-loving elite. I'm telling you, this could solve your financial woes and then some."

There was no way she'd find the time. "I'll think about it."

"We'll talk details later. I'll forward the info via email."

"I appreciate it. And you, for thinking of me."

"Anytime. Now go show those small-town folks what you're made of."

Drake exited the store, once again with his sons in hand. They each sucked on a lollipop bigger than their mouths. Those would keep them occupied for a while.

Drake caught her gaze, held it and grinned.

Causing her stomach to do an odd flip.

She quickly looked away. "Thanks, Toni. I'll try." She'd be happy to leave with her dignity—and heart—intact. Their conversation at the work site this morning had been much too pleasant, enough to make her wonder if maybe he wasn't such a creep, after all.

Regardless, she had no intention of falling for a small-town cowboy—or his cute kids.

Maybe if she told herself that often enough, her ricocheting emotions would follow suit.

Chapter Seven

Drake held tight to his wiggly little ones and followed Faith across the street to a small store sandwiched between a Laundromat and a tattoo shop. Various shapes and sizes of stained glass designs decorated the windows, and panels of white tile with redbrick lettering framed the door.

Sheets of expensive glass and a pair of energetic rascals… He and the boys should have waited in the car, except they'd been sitting long enough.

Faith pushed inside, triggering a bell.

The boys lurched after her, but he pulled them back and squatted at eye level with them. "Got to mind your manners in there. You hear me?"

They nodded, still squirming.

"And absolutely no touching—or no ice cream. Got it?"

They gave him two more nods, their expressions serious.

"All right then." A musty scent tickled Drake's nose as he stepped inside, and stale air swirled around him. Irish folk music pinged from an old radio on a brown filing cabinet topped with paper, a canister of deodorant spray and a box of tissues. Various glass trinkets decorated a center aisle and dangled from twine tacked to the ceiling.

Well out of the boys' reach.

"Be there in a minute," a male voice called from somewhere in the back.

"No rush." Faith strolled toward a wall of cubbies filled with sheets of glass.

Drake stood back, monitoring his kids while watching her pull out various colors. With each one, she ran her hands along the smooth surface, head cocked, as if deep in thought. He'd seen that expression numerous times back at the church, when she'd been working on something. Almost like she'd slipped into her own little world.

This was clearly her domain, and never had she looked more beautiful. Except maybe the afternoon he'd caught her sitting on a rock at the work site, with the sun behind her, filtering through her chestnut hair. Her cheeks were flushed from the Texas humidity, giving her an almost childlike vulnerability.

And stirring feelings he'd be wise not to entertain. They came from completely different worlds, separated by almost two hours of hard asphalt. He'd never been a fan of long-distance relationships, especially when his kids were involved, which they'd have to be if anything became serious between him and Faith.

He could never leave Sage Creek—take his boys away from their grandparents, their aunt and church family.

But if Faith moved there...

"Isn't this interesting?"

Her soft voice averted his thoughts, and, William in tow, he shoved his free hand in his pocket and ambled over. Her faint floral scent spiked his pulse, giving him brain freeze.

She tilted her face, and her eyes intensified as they met his. What would it feel like to run his fingers through her long, satiny hair?

"Sorry to keep you..."

She spun around. "Thomas, hi."

Spell broken, Drake took a deep breath and tipped his hat at the frowning man walking toward them. He was tall, had a long, shaggy beard shaved down the middle, and an Adam's apple that could put Ichabod Crane to shame.

The guy's gaze swept over Drake, as if sizing him up, before shifting to Faith. With a stiff smile, he embraced her. "Good to see you." He eyed Drake over her shoulder.

"Same." She stepped back, her grin widening.

"Drake, this is my dear friend Thomas Downing. He and his father own this place." She introduced Drake and explained his role in the restoration.

The two shook hands.

"Nice to meet you." The man's puckered face contradicted his words.

William tugged free of Drake's grip and plopped onto the floor. Making an engine noise, he drove his favorite toy car, the one he always kept in his pocket, back and forth across a line in the carpet. Hopefully that would occupy him for a bit. His older brother seemed content to look at all the vases and whatnot.

Faith fingered a glass feather hanging from a metal tree. "Want us to pull around back?"

"Sure, once we settle things up." He set an invoice on the counter. "I must have an old card on file. The charges were declined."

"Oh, no." Her eyes widened. "You serious? You should've said something."

"No biggie. I figured we could take care of things once you got here, considering how long we've been doing business together."

"I appreciate that." She handed over a credit card.

"Uh…" Thomas glanced from the card to the paper in front of him, then back to the card. "That's the one I have on file."

"Maybe you entered the numbers wrong?"

He shook his head. "Tried it four times."

The poor girl's face paled about two shades. Then, crossing her arms, she turned to Drake. "I was going to pay and submit the receipt to your insurance agency, but this is probably easier." She held out her hand, palm up.

"No problem." He pulled his wallet from his back pocket and stepped to the counter. "I'm sure this'll count toward my deductible, anyway." Regardless, he was responsible for all expenses related to the accident.

Faith gave a curt nod and moved aside. "It's Drake's fault I had to place this order." She relayed the details of the accident, and the man's features shifted into a smirk.

As if to say "So you wouldn't be here with Faith, acting all chummy, otherwise."

The truth stung much more than it should have.

He and Faith had no future together. That was as clear as those fancy glass sheets filling the cubby beside him. Besides, he hardly knew the girl.

But he hadn't felt so intrigued by a lady since he first met his sweet Lydia. He hadn't once thought of dating since he lost her.

Did this mean he was ready to love again?

"Thanks, Thomas." Faith gave her friend a hug. "I appreciate how quickly you got these or-

dered for me. You literally saved the restoration."
And potentially her career.

"No problem." He shifted his focus to Drake,
as if trying to place him. Or maybe he was worried about Faith climbing back in his truck,
considering the reason for her reorder. Thomas
always had a tendency to be protective. The big
brother she'd always wanted.

When he focused on her once again, his smile
returned, though stiffer than normal. "Best of
luck. Make sure to stop in when you get back in
town. I'll hook you up with some sick discounts.
We can talk textures and technique over coffee."

"Sounds great."

He eyed Drake one more time, gave a parting
wave and went back inside.

Seated in the back, the boys started whining
for ice cream. Drake's attempts to quiet them
proved ineffective.

Faith scrutinized her newly purchased sheets
of glass, lying in Drake's pickup bed. Though
still in their packaging and cushioned by a fair
amount of bubble wrap, they weren't nearly as
secure as those she'd loaded into her trailer.

She scraped her teeth across her bottom lip.
"You sure they'll be all right back there?"

"My dad's lug nuts are good and tight." He
winked, his blue eyes sparkling. "And I'll drive
slow."

He opened her door for her, then stood with his

hand on the roof, his tall, muscular frame block-ing the sun. The familiar scent of his aftershave ignited her pulse.

He extended a hand, and she swallowed, her mouth suddenly dry. After a moment's hesita-tion, she allowed him to help her in, his palm rough and callused against her skin.

"Thank you." Her voice came out hoarse. Blushing, she looked away.

She was much more comfortable with Drake the cocky jerk. This gentler version left her off-kilter and reacting in ways she had no intention of analyzing.

"My pleasure." He shut her door and rounded the front end of the vehicle, drumming his hands on the hood en route. He slid in next to her, cranked the engine and glanced at the dash. "Look at the time. No wonder the boys are hungry. Any must-eats up this way? With ice cream nearby, of course." He shot her a wink that caused her heart to stutter.

As if in response, her stomach growled, add-ing heat to her face. "Um…"

The man and his kids were hungry, nothing more. It would be polite to show them a uniquely Austin restaurant.

Two colleagues sitting across from each other. Making eye contact. Talking.

With a couple of squirmy kids between them. That'd keep things casual enough.

As long as they went somewhere low-key, somewhere visually distracting, loud, even, everything would be fine.

She fastened her seat belt. "How about barbecue? There's this fun place downtown."

"Let's do it." He eased onto the frontage road and cast her a sidelong glance. "You and Thomas—you been friends for a while?"

"About five years. He's a good guy, always helpful, and never in a hurry to get people out of his shop. He runs classes on Saturdays, and sometimes hosts fun socials on Friday nights. It's a great way for the art community to get together."

"I heard Austin's pretty artsy."

"This your first time visiting the city?"

"Yep."

"But you live so close."

He merged onto I-35, heading south. "I tend to hit Houston whenever I need something I can't get in Sage Creek, which isn't often."

"You're kidding, right? You're what, thirty-five?"

One side of his mouth quirked up. "Thirty-one. For three more months."

"All right. Thirty-one, and you've never taken a trip to your state's capital?"

"Guess I'm content where I'm at."

Content. Faith couldn't remember the last time she'd felt that way. Then again, her art career was dying, her funds rapidly depleting, and she was on the cusp of becoming the failure her father always predicted she'd be.

A squeaky voice drew Faith's attention to the boys. They shared an iPad between them. Trevor bobbed his head in time to a song about shaking one's sillies out. Faith hid a giggle with her hand.

"Tell me about this place we're going to." Drake stopped at a red light. "Does it fit with the slogan Keep Austin Weird?"

She laughed. "I guess you'll have to wait and see."

For the remainder of the drive, the oldest kept them all occupied with knock-knock jokes that made no sense. By the time they pulled into a downtown parking garage near the restaurant, her jittery nerves had settled some.

"Wait." Drake raised a finger to his kids and stepped out. He rounded the pickup bed, making his way toward her. She scampered out before he could reach her, refusing to allow any more of his Southern gentlemen charm. It was severely challenging her resolve.

He moved to the rear door, unbuckled William and tossed him over his shoulder. William squealed and wiggled his feet.

Trevor ran toward the street, but Drake caught him by the wrist. "Walk." When the child complied, Drake released him and inhaled. "If that smell's coming from Cooper's, I s'pect we're in for quite a meal."

"They've got the best pit-smoked meat around."

"My kind of place."

"Your kids going to be okay here?"

"Yep. I'll get 'em some ribs and a bowl of ice cream, and they'll be happy as colts in the oat bin."

Little William scurried to her side and grabbed her hand. She startled, then smiled. Such a precious little one. She felt a sudden urge to scoop him up and kiss those chubby cheeks.

Instead, she led him and the others past a group of tourists gathered around a map to the old-fashioned, rustic barbecue place. Sandwiched between a corner bodega and a hotel, Cooper's wood siding and countrified signage stood out and screamed Wild West.

When they stepped inside, the temperature decreased about ten degrees, sending a shiver through her.

Hand in his pocket, Drake looked around. "Nice."

She followed his gaze from the brick walls and cement floors to the long, cowhide bench lining the wall behind them. Various wooden signs, the kind one might see on hiking trails, were tacked to a pillar to their left. Arrows pointed every which way—upstairs, to the event room, restrooms. One simply said Hey, Y'all. Three exclamation marks followed.

"We order there." She pointed to the meat counter up ahead, manned by a guy wearing a ball cap and long red apron. "Everything's sold by the pound."

"Awesome."

Ten minutes later, they carried their trays of food, ice cream included, to one of the many picnic style tables with bench seating. Thankfully, Drake had insisted on paying for hers. Though it had stung, with her credit card maxed out, she couldn't afford restaurant food.

She really needed that magazine feature in *Lone Star Gems*. In case the art show didn't pan out, which, considering she had yet to work on anything, was likely.

Drake sat between his boys. "I like this place."

"I haven't been here in years." She sat across from him and forked through her jalapeño mac and cheese—a dish she'd been wanting to try.

"Mmm." Drake took a bite of ribs dripping with barbecue sauce and closed his eyes. "Almost as good as my grandmother used to make."

"Used to?"

"She's been gone going on five years now."

"Oh. I'm sorry."

"She went in her sleep. The doctors think she died of cardiac arrest, but her heart broke long before that when she lost my granddaddy."

"Your family's close, aren't they?"

"Yep. Like they say, a man who can't count on his blood relatives is in pretty sorry shape."

"Right." She frowned, thinking of the last time she'd asked her parents for anything. She should probably give them both a call.

William started to climb down from his bench seat.

Drake grabbed him by the waist. "Hold on, little fella. How about you and your brother make some paper-towel airplanes? See if you can't figure out a way to make them fly. Think you can do that?" He snagged a few sheets from the roll in the center of the table, handed some to each child. "Trevor, think you can help your brother out here?"

Trevor nodded and set to work.

"So—" Faith dabbed her mouth with her napkin "—what was it like growing up on a ranch?"

"Busy. Seemed there was always something needing to be done. Fences to fix. Ornery bulls chasing after our younger heifers to divert."

She laughed. "Really?"

He nodded. "Can't breed the females until they're at least a year old. Otherwise they could die on us—them and the baby." He squirted some ketchup onto his potato salad, making her wince. "Plus we—I mean, my dad—grows his own feed, so there's the crops to tend to, horses to care for."

Her heart skipped. "You've got horses?"

Amusement lit his eyes. "Four. You're a horse gal, I take it?"

"Not exactly. I mean, I've always loved them. I was the typical, dreamy-eyed little girl who asked for a pony every Christmas."

"Ever been riding?"

She shook her head.

"Guess we've got to fix that then, don't we?"

Why did her stomach suddenly launch into acrobatics?

He took a sip of his drink. "You got plans this weekend?"

"Other than staring at my hotel room walls?" She gave a nervous laugh. His offer appealed to her much more than was prudent. And she really did need to work on something for the Honey Locust showing. But there was no reason she couldn't do both. Who knew when she'd have another opportunity like this?

To ride a horse. Her enthusiasm had nothing to do with the handsome cowboy.

Regardless of her ricocheting pulse.

"Who knows?" He scooped up a forkful of potato salad. "The quiet, relaxed pace of Sage Creek just might grow on you."

Unfortunately, it was already starting to. Or at least, one of its residents was. That was the problem. One she needed to cut off now, before entangling herself in a big, emotional mess. Not only were she and Drake as different as trees and cement, but the guy had kids. She had no intention of playing mom to someone else's little ones. Regardless of how adorable and sweet they were.

Chapter Eight

The next morning, Drake herded his kids into his truck and headed to his parents' ranch. He'd wanted to stop by the day before but his trip to Austin had eaten up almost the entire day.

Not that he'd minded exactly. He smiled, remembering the way Faith had lingered in the glass shop, running her hands along the various sheets, her pretty little head tilted. The way she'd engaged his kids. Then at the barbecue place, her shy, furtive glances and her childlike blush when he'd offered to take her horseback riding.

Too bad things could never work out between the two of them.

With "Baby Beluga" playing through his speakers, per William's request, Drake turned onto the long, gravel road leading to his parents' ranch.

What in blazes…?

He slowed and shook his head. His mom was attempting to chase a heifer out of their alfalfa fields.

"Hold up, boys." He put his truck in Park.

"What happened?" Trevor asked. "Can we come?"

"No." Drake didn't need two boys and a cow running lose in a field. "Now sit tight." He got out, maneuvered over the sagging barbed wire lining the road, and jogged through the dew-dampened vegetation toward his mom.

She turned to him with wide eyes shadowed by purplish bags. Looked like she was still having trouble sleeping. Not that he expected otherwise, with all she had to manage with the ranch, Dad and their rapidly mounting medical debt.

He eyed the cow. "How long she been out here?"

"I'm not sure." There was no telling how much the animal had eaten. Hopefully not enough to bloat her stomach and kill her.

They'd know soon enough, unfortunately. "Let me grab a feed bucket to coax her out of here." He hurried to the barn and back.

Bucket in hand, he moved in closer and signaled his mom to close in on the cow's other side. He jiggled the grain to make a swishing sound. "Come on, ol' girl."

The cow's ears pricked, and she started walking his way.

Drake stepped back toward the fence. His mom followed.

He gazed toward the pastures. "Dillon working today?" He was the only ranch hand his folks had kept on since Dad's accident. Though they needed the extra help now more than ever, they didn't have the money for salaries.

"Yea, to help with calving. A couple of mommas are ready to birth anytime. I wanted him here, in case of problems."

"Smart." It seemed at least one catastrophe hit every calving season. "I'll call him in a bit. Tell him to watch this little lady for signs of bloating."

As they guided the cow back to where she belonged, they found a partially uprooted fence post and splintered boards. The animal had probably been leaning against the rotting wood when it had given way.

He scanned the area, then closed up the fence opening as best he could. At least, far as he could see, none of the other cattle had wandered out. "I'll get this patched up right quick."

He'd need to replace the three broken boards and probably the post, as well. That'd take a chunk of time.

Time he'd planned to spend riding horses with Faith. But he could come out early, put in a few hours at the ranch and have the evening free.

Why was he planning his day around that woman? She'd be gone by month's end. There was no sense starting something he couldn't finish. And for sure he didn't want his kids growing attached. But he'd already made the invitation and she'd accepted. A man needed to follow through. Besides, he couldn't send her back to the city without having been on a horse.

"We appreciate all your help, your dad and I." His mom wrapped an arm around his waist and gave a gentle squeeze. "I know you've got a lot on your hands, with the restoration project and—"

"Family first. You know that."

She teared up. "What would we do without you? You're a good kid."

He laughed. Going on thirty-two with kids of his own, and still she called him a kid. "Walk with me to the truck. I'll give you a ride to the house."

By eight thirty, he and his little men had bellies full of gravy and biscuits, he'd helped get his dad up and into his wheelchair and his boys were playing with his old plastic army set in the living room.

He ruffled William's hair and gave Trevor a fist bump. "I best get going before the crew thinks I've ditched."

"Here." His mom handed him two thermoses and two paper lunch bags. "Take these with you. For you and Faith. And invite her to church tonight. No sense her sitting in that hotel room all by herself."

"Uh…" He rubbed the back of his neck. He was becoming more entangled with that woman by the minute, when what he needed was increased distance.

"My stars." His mother held a hand to her chest. "I never thought I'd see the day. But it's about time."

"What?"

She offered a knowing smile. "I'm glad to see you're jumping back in the saddle. You've been keeping to yourself for far too long now."

"You're way off. Faith and I are coworkers. That's it."

"Uh-huh. And that's why your eyes sparked when I mentioned her. Like they used to whenever I'd bring out chocolate chip cookies. I know my boy." She grabbed his hand. "This is a good thing, son."

"Don't get your hopes up, Mom. Soon as the restoration project's done, she'll be hightailing it back to Austin."

"So convince her to stay."

His heart gave a jolt. But his mom's notion was ridiculous. He and Faith were from two different worlds, and she'd made it clear what she thought of his. Of him period, though she did appear to be warming up some. Regardless, he didn't have the time to pursue a woman, nor did he have any intention of chasing after some city girl.

Faith straightened and stretched. She inspected the stained glass window she'd been working on. Unbroken, it had just needed a good cleaning. It always struck her how vivid the colors appeared once all the dirt and residue had been scrubbed away.

She needed some fresh air. Grabbing her backpack from the floor, she headed outside to her favorite break spot—a stump at the edge of the church property. Shaded by a mature oak, it gave her a quiet place to think and, hopefully, find inspiration for Honey Locust's private showing.

She opened the paper bag Drake had brought for her and peered inside. His mother had made a sandwich, apple slices and some kind of cookie. She pulled it out, thinking back to her time with Drake at the Austin restaurant. When they'd made plans to go horseback riding.

Why hadn't she told him no?

Her phone rang. She pulled it from her back pocket and frowned. Why was her roommate calling? "Hello?"

"Hi. How's Sage Creek?"

"Hot and humid. What's up?" It wasn't like Jenna, an introvert in the extreme, to chitchat or make unnecessary phone calls.

Her pause made Faith uneasy.

"So, um… I lost my job."

Faith blinked. "What? Why? When?"

"It's a long story, but let's just say I blew it big time."

"Wow. I'm so sorry. What're you going to do?"

Jenna sighed. "Move back home."

Faith's mouth went dry. Would she bail on her rent? At least their lease was almost up, but…

There was no way Faith could keep her apartment without a roommate, and with her credit—and rapidly shrinking bank account—she held little chance of finding another one. Plus she'd be out her deposit thanks to a massive coffee stain smack-dab in the center of the living room carpet.

"I'm sorry," Jenna said. "I know this stinks. For both of us."

Faith rubbed her face. "It happens." Now what? She didn't have time to worry about this, nor could she put it off. If she didn't figure out something soon, in a month she'd be following in Jenna's footsteps, something Faith refused to do.

She ended the call and dropped her phone on the grass by her feet.

"Everything all right?"

Drake's deep, Southern voice quickened her pulse. She looked up to find him standing a few feet away, watching her with a furrowed brow.

"It will be."

He studied her a moment longer, then gave a

quick nod, as if he didn't believe her but, mercifully, wasn't going to push. "How's your lunch?"

"I haven't tried it yet, but it looks amazing." Much better than her stale jerky, which she could now save for dinner. She didn't have a dime to waste.

"I figured you might be needing my help again. With lifting."

"Oh. Um… Sure. If you've got time."

"Yep."

She took a gulp of water, then led the way back to the hot and stuffy shed, where five windows soaked, three waiting to be scrubbed and two others to be repaired. They picked up one that was finished and resting against a wall. Then, together, they proceeded to the side of the church where he'd already positioned the scaffolding.

"Hey, Billy." He called out to a guy pushing a wheelbarrow of broken boards toward the dumpster. "Help us out here?"

The man gave a quick nod and sauntered over.

"Faith and I will climb up, and you can hand us the glass."

"Yes, sir." He took the window from Drake, and Faith slowly released her grip. This was the hardest part of the restoration project—entrusting her work to the potentially slippery and shaky hands of another.

"Be careful." She let out a slow breath. "It's very fragile."

"Yes, ma'am."

The three of them lifted the window, then Billy left Faith and Drake to fit the glass back into position.

"There you two are." Lucy wobbled toward them in three-inch heels.

Drake shifted to face her. "What can we do for you?"

"I know it's late notice, but we've scheduled an impromptu meeting for tonight at six. In the high school cafeteria. The team would like you both to be there."

Impromptu or emergency? Had they managed to get their bids all straightened out and decided they didn't want Faith on this project, after all? Surely they wouldn't do that now, almost two days in. Besides, they'd signed a contract.

Unless there was fine print, a loophole she'd failed to notice...

"I'll be there," Drake said.

"Me, too." She forced a confident smile. She was probably worrying over nothing. She had a tendency to do that, especially when money was tight.

"You're going to regret this." Her dad's oft-spoken statement, ever since she'd told him she wanted to drop out of college to pursue art, re-surfaced. It was time she proved him wrong.

Lucy made small talk for a while, then thanked them for their hard work and left.

"I'll climb down first." Drake descended, then stabilized the scaffolding so Faith could do the same. "You got any more windows ready to go in?"

"Not yet. I'm doing them in shifts, soaking some while I scrub and repair others."

"Just let me know."

"I will, thanks." She had a feeling he'd meander her way long before she went looking for him.

Was he trying to be considerate or was he checking up on her work? Did he still think she was the wrong person for the job?

Didn't matter. She was here to complete a restoration, not please handsome, nosy cowboys.

Decked out in the equivalent of hazmat gear, Drake spent the rest of the morning in the attic helping his guys shovel out massive quantities of bat guano. Based on the growing pile of fragmented wood, they'd lost a chunk of flooring or wall also.

Was he frustrated? Behind schedule?

Like she would be if she didn't step things up. Lucy and the mayor expected the project to be completed by Settler's Day. Seventeen more windows needed deep cleaning and ten others had shattered pieces she needed to cut and replace.

She'd work on some of the more simple designs first. Then she'd tackle the window with the intricate image of Jesus surrounded by a group of children. With its background of clouds in a blue sky, framed in a border of vines and flowers, that one would take time and skill.

She tapped her marker against her chin—those colors, and the way the girl in the forefront's robe rippled… She could envision a multilayered mosaic with similar hues, but instead of ancient Palestinians, she'd include…

A cowboy. She smiled, nearly laughing out loud. That would be hilarious, but she doubted it'd get into the Honey Locust's private showing. Unless…

Something uniquely Texas, with an historical flair… An image of an old photograph she'd seen in one of her restoration books came to mind. It was a black-and-white picture of a man in a straw hat and loose coveralls, leaning against an old tractor, the setting sun framing him. It was a brilliant piece that captured a feeling of nostalgia and simplicity.

What if she painted an acrylic of Drake, bent over one of the pews, his cowboy hat tilted? Maybe with him sanding it. Or…building one. She'd show just his profile, with his facial features shaded. He'd symbolize all the unknown laborers who'd poured their hearts into this and countless other churches across the state.

She grinned. That just might work.

She'd sketch it out tonight. Maybe try to snap a picture of him as he worked this afternoon.

As if she needed yet another reason to think about the man.

It was time for a break. A short walk would get the blood flowing through her legs and clear her head of handsome yet unattainable cowboys.

She dried her stiff hands on a towel and traipsed down a narrow path dissecting the patchy lawn. About five hundred feet to her right, a couple of tall, lanky teenagers worked on tearing up sections of dead grass. The landscape looked like one big brown blotch with tufts of green sprinkled in. One good rain would turn it all into a giant mud puddle.

Drake's boys would love that.

Strange that she'd think of them, although they were pretty adorable.

As was their father, unfortunately.

Pushing the thought aside, she strode to a dented cooler a few feet from someone's truck. She grabbed her third water bottle for the day and ambled into the sanctuary to see how Drake's crew was progressing.

Purely out of curiosity, and to witness the restoration of history firsthand. Not to see him.

She paused near the baptismal to admire a mural behind it. Palm trees, birds nestled in the branches. Ivy climbed up the trunks, and flowering bushes filled the space beneath.

She knew from articles she'd read that many of the images she saw held symbolic meaning.

There was a pelican, said to sacrifice itself to care for its young. An anchor spoke of hope. Every brushstroke seemed to tell a story.

Perhaps that was what she loved most about historical churches. It was something she tried to do with her own art. Whether anyone else understood the meaning was irrelevant. Her heart knew, and it was from her heart that she created.

She had turned to leave when her eye caught on an oblong patch of white. Was that…?

She stepped closer and ran her hand along the mural, her fingers lingering over a slight indentation. Leaning forward, she squinted. Not good. It appeared the walls had been restored once before. The committee wouldn't be pleased. Not with how badly they wanted this church listed in the historic registry. Nor with how tight their funds were.

Something like this could absolutely derail the project, and put the entire town in an uproar, Drake included.

Chapter Nine

By four o'clock, Faith was beat and covered in sweat and grime, and the humidity had turned her wavy hair frizzy. This wasn't how she wanted to greet the cultural committee.

Had she known about this little meeting ahead of time, she would've brought a change of clothes.

She headed for the bathroom to freshen up, reaching the church as Drake was walking out.

His gaze latched on to hers. "You ready?"

She felt her cheeks flush at the thought of sitting beside him in his truck, alone. Which was ridiculous, considering she'd done so a few times before. But that was back when she'd thought he was a jerk. This new Drake she kept catching glimpses of left her unsettled in the most unwelcome way.

She swallowed. "I, uh…" She was acting like a tongue-tied teenager. So she'd seen a nicer side of the guy. He was simply treating her like a professional. "Give me ten minutes?"

"Sure thing."

She continued inside with the distinct feeling that he was watching her. She'd caught him doing so numerous times throughout the day.

Almost as if…

She shook the thought aside and hurried to the tiny, two-stall bathroom in the back. When she returned, Drake was waiting in a new, fresh shirt, wiping his face with a wet rag.

He'd cleaned up. For her?

No. He'd probably sweated through the last one and, like her, wanted to look somewhat presentable for the meeting.

He beat her to his truck and stood with the passenger's side door open.

Ever the gentleman.

"Thank you." If only her emotions would show the same nonchalance that—she hoped—her calm demeanor did.

He engaged the engine, and the radio came on, tuned to the local country station. A throaty voice belted out something about dead-end jobs, unpaid bills and a broken-down vehicle. It was like listening to a recap of her life.

She buckled her seat belt. "So stereotypical. Next he'll be singing about prayers that don't get answered and the girl who ran off with someone else."

"Not a fan of country music, I take it."

"Hardly."

"What do you listen to?"

"You'd laugh."

"Probably. Tell me anyway."

"A little bit of everything. Nat King Cole, the Talking Heads, Aerosmith."

"That's quite a playlist."

"You asked."

His easy smile made her feel off-kilter. "That I did."

Not five minutes later, they found themselves stuck on the wrong side of a freight train.

Drake's engine clicked, then settled into a low hum.

He drummed his fingers on the steering wheel. "So, how long you been doing art?"

"Restoration, you mean?"

He gave a slight shrug. "That and at that studio you work for—the one in Austin."

"I've been creating things for as long as I can remember. Drawing, pottery. I took my first glassblowing class my freshman year in college, and I fell in love. It's been my favorite medium ever since."

"You got your own furnace?"

So the guy knew a thing or two about art. Interesting. "No, but there's one about ten miles from me. At a co-op called the Red Rock Firing Whole."

"Interesting name."

She smiled. "They're an interesting group. Hippies with a gothic-slash-techno flair…"

He gave a slow nod.

"What about you?" She tried to see the end of the train. It looked like they'd be sitting for a while. Not good. The last thing she wanted to do was show up late for the meeting. "Do you often work on historic buildings?"

"I'm the town handyman. I fix roofs, drywall, put up fences. You name it."

So he wasn't even in the restoration business. And he'd dinged her for lack of experience?

"I help out at the church when I have time. Been tackling their bat problem since we first discovered the critters last winter. That's been a process. It's illegal to fumigate them. You got to seal off their entrances without trapping them inside, and wait until all their babies are born."

She grimaced. "I'd rather not hear the details."

He laughed. "No problem." The final four cars chugged by, and the railroad barricade lifted. "'Bout time."

Drake weaved his way through a residential neighborhood to a single-story brick building. The sign in front said Sage Creek High School. Centered in an oblong patch of browning grass, it had a flat roof, red trim and long wooden benches flanking the entrance.

Based on the handful of vehicles parked in

the lot, Faith guessed the cultural committee waited inside.

Did they plan to let her go? Had they run out of funds and needed to abort the project?

Why did she always jump to the worst-case scenarios?

She took a deep breath, squelched her anxious thoughts and stepped out into the muggy afternoon sun.

Once again, Drake reached the entrance ahead of her and opened the door wide.

She was becoming much too familiar with this gentlemanly gesture—and his lazy grin. "Thank you." As she entered, a swirl of cold air sent goose bumps up her arms.

The florescent lighting reflected off the checked linoleum. On the wall across from them, a display case held four trophies of varying sizes.

"This way." Drake motioned for her to follow him around the corner and down a short hall lined with classroom doors.

Their footfalls echoed off the cement walls, and soon voices merged with them. After another turn, they reached an area lined with rectangular tables with attached bench seating. The cultural committee sat at one near the center. Heads swiveled their direction as they entered, and a few people stood to greet them.

"Howdy." Drake removed his hat, then sauntered across the room to shake hands with a couple of men before taking a seat near the end.

Faith followed and sat across from him. The mayor, whom she'd met twice, occupied a chair he'd pulled to the head of the table.

He tugged on one end of his horseshoe mustache. "Drake. Ms. Nichols. Thanks for coming." His gaze dropped to an opened file folder in front of him.

She couldn't help feeling as if she'd stumbled back into junior high—the new girl in the cafeteria edging up to the cool gang.

Who, for all she knew, were about to send her packing.

The man to Faith's left shifted. Someone coughed.

The mayor folded his hands in front of him. "How're things going with the restoration?"

They wanted an update? Was that all this was about?

"Things are progressing." Drake scratched the back of his neck. "No major hiccups or unexpecteds."

"Good." The mayor shifted his attention to Faith.

She straightened. "Everything's going according to plan on my end." Minus the fact that it was taking her longer than anticipated to remove all the windows, but she'd make up that time no problem.

"Glad to hear it." The mayor's mustache tugging became more pronounced.

"Although…" She took a deep breath and released it slowly. "There is something we should discuss."

The mayor paused midtug. "All right."

She explained the peeling paint she'd discovered and what it meant. "I know we're under a tight time line, but I also know you hope to get the church declared a historic landmark."

"You think it'd be best if we restored the murals to their original state?"

Murmurs rippled down either side of the table.

"Now wait a minute." Drake's deep voice silenced everyone. "That church has looked the same for as long as most folks can remember. As far as I'm concerned, that's historic enough. Way I see it, that patch could mean nothing. Who's to say there weren't layers originally? Artists do that, or maybe things were restored exactly. Or close enough to."

Silence. A short, potbellied man kitty-corner to Faith started popping his knuckles.

The mayor rubbed the back of his hand. "Lucy?"

"I'm not sure. But I think it'd be helpful to stay as close to the original as possible—if we have the time and resources. Martha, you've been working on the historical details more closely than I have." She addressed a tiny woman with short black hair.

"Honestly, at this point, the historic registry might be the least of our concerns," Martha answered.

That didn't sound good.

Lucy nodded and fiddled with her bracelet. "I agree. A project of this size requires a great deal of funding." She looked at the mayor, as if wanting him to take over. With an almost unperceivable sigh, she continued. "Insurance helps, but we've got a pretty high deductible. This is something our team discussed at length, before hiring the both of you. Matter of fact, Martha's been working on grant proposals since the fire occurred."

Faith released the breath she'd been holding. Good. Very good.

"Unfortunately..." Lucy looked at Faith. "We received notice this morning that one we'd been counting on fell through."

A wave of nausea gripped her. "What does—" Her voice came out squeaky. She cleared her throat. "What does that mean?"

The mayor closed his file folder and pushed it aside. "We need to figure out a way to raise funds."

That involved her and Drake how? Surely they didn't think she'd join their fund-raising efforts.

She wasn't the spaghetti supper, bake sale kind of girl.

"We've got numerous ideas in the works…" Lucy rested her forearms on the table. "How would you both like to be in our Fourth of July parade? We've landed on a great idea for the float this year—a jailhouse, with bars and all. And the two of you locked behind them."

She went on to explain how townspeople would buy raffle tickets to pay for their release, but Faith was barely listening. She was stuck on the idea of being dressed in prison garb and paraded through the streets of Sage Creek.

Lucy's grin stretched about two inches too wide. "What do you say?"

"Uh…" Faith's cheeks felt ready to combust. "I…"

Drake chuckled. "Leave it to y'all to come up with the wackiest ideas. If this'll get our church back up and running, I'm in."

"Great." The mayor slapped his hand on the table, making Faith jump. "Now that it's settled, you two are free to go."

Faith blinked. How had that happened?

"All right then." Drake stood, placed his Stetson back on his head and turned to Faith. "I 'spect we should get back to it."

Images of herself wearing a baggy, black-and-white-striped jumpsuit—while locked in close quarters with Drake Owens—filled her mind.

And yet she couldn't back out now. Not without looking like a complete jerk.

She stumbled to her feet.

"Wait." Lucy struggled to untangle herself from between the bench and table. "About that paint patch." Her wedge sandals smacked the linoleum as she caught up to Faith. "I know you did a fair amount of research, before putting in your bid."

She nodded.

"You didn't happen to uncover any old photographs, did you? That might show the church's interior?"

"Some. But most of what I found weren't very clear. Besides, I focused more on the windows."

"I see." She scrunched her lips to one side. "I'll work on gathering some up, then. This town has enough hoarders to keep the best antique shoppers busy for decades." She laughed. "Could you help us look through them? I know you're a history buff, and with your artistic eye, well, I think you'd be better at this than us."

Sift through generations of preserved historical material? What an opportunity! "I'd love to."

"I'll join you."

She startled at Drake's sudden and rather forceful voice. What was his motivation? "If you want."

He gave a quick nod.

That meant they'd be spending even more time together, something she both looked forward to…and dreaded.

Chapter Ten

Drake paused outside the cafeteria to check the time on his phone. "Church'll be starting soon."

Faith's steps halted. "What? On a Wednesday?"

"Midweek prayer service, though ours is more like a casual Bible study. We meet here, till the renovations are finished. Folks should be…"

Giggling drifted toward them, and the patter of small footsteps echoed down the narrow hall.

Drake grinned. His boys.

A moment later, the two came barreling toward them.

"Faith!" His littlest ran straight to her, his favorite dump truck in one hand and his tattered blue blanket in the other.

Faith's face lit up. "Hey, little guy. What do you have there?"

"Pile twuck." He dropped to his knees and pushed it in a wide arc with a *vroom.* "Like Daddy."

"Nice."

She greeted his oldest with a smile, then, lowering to eye level, returned her attention to William, listening patiently as he relayed a story about a lizard he'd found climbing up the porch railing. She and Drake exchanged a glance, and the laughter in her eyes, as if his little man brought her joy, stalled his breath.

"Hey, Mr. Builder Man." He tickled William's side, then ruffled his oldest's hair. "Sounds like you two had a good day."

Trevor shrugged, his frown so dramatic Drake could hardly keep from laughing. "Aunt Elizabeth made me read a bunch of books."

"Two." Having reached them, his sister grinned, first at him, then Faith. "Hey, girl."

"Hi." Faith straightened, glanced down the hall, then gave his sister an almost shaky smile. Poor thing always seemed a bit jittery, like she'd been caught on a ledge without a safety harness. Was she stressed about the restoration project? She'd certainly tangled things up, with all that paint-patch talk. Something Leaded Pane never would've done.

Then again, he couldn't fault her for being observant. Neither could he let her convince folks to change the look of the church.

Elizabeth looped an arm through Faith's and started to lead her toward the gym. "I'm so glad you decided to come tonight. I would've invited you but didn't have your phone number. We should fix that."

The twinge of jealousy that shot through Drake caught him off guard.

He turned back to his boys to find them racing down the other end of the hall. Trevor had little William's blanket, and his brother was chasing after him. Looked like they had energy to burn. Did that mean they'd spent the day inside?

Kids needed to be out running amuck and... watching their Pop-Pop work the ranch.

His dad's accident had changed everything. If only Drake had stayed to help that day. And now, in the middle of fighting toward recovery, but buried by medical bills, he and Mom risked losing everything.

Drake couldn't let that happen.

He just needed to figure something out. Soon.

Where were his parents? Elizabeth didn't say anything about them staying home. He again checked the time on his phone.

Whiny shouts drew his attention to his rambunctious boys.

Trevor stood against the far wall, holding his brother's wadded blanket just out of reach. William jumped for it. He missed and flung himself on the floor with a wail.

"All right, now. Give me..." Taking it would only upset William more. And man, could that boy carry on once something pricked his temper. He'd probably make a fuss all through church.

Drake shot his oldest a stern look. "Give your brother back his blanket."

"You said he's not supposed to have it."

That battle was lost the minute Elizabeth had handed the thing over. She must've driven back to his house after he'd dropped the kids off this morning. She coddled those boys. He'd have a talk with her about that later.

"Come on." He wiped away one of William's tears and gave him a gentle punch to his shoulder. "You don't want to miss the singing, do you?" The little boy could belt out a hymn like no one else.

William sniffled and shook his head.

Once in the gym, Drake removed his hat and scanned the bleachers filled with smiling, jabbering faces for a glimpse of Faith. She and his sister sat three rows up on the far left. Elizabeth was gabbing, like always.

Faith seemed to have relaxed some. At least her eyes weren't about to bug out of her head anymore. But she kept rubbing her arm, while casting frequent glances toward Pastor Roger. Her wavy hair framed her delicate, sun-kissed face in loose ringlets. She was by far the prettiest woman in the room.

Maybe he should sit by her. Help put her at ease some.

Or would she take that wrong? Think he was flirting with her?

If she didn't live in another city…

Why was he even thinking like that?

"Drake."

He cringed inwardly and turned at Sally Jo's overly sweet—like overripe prunes—voice. "Howdy."

"I feel like I haven't seen you in forever." She hardly ever came to Wednesday night prayer service. "How's your daddy?"

"All right." At least, as much as could be expected. But Drake wasn't looking to start an in-depth conversation with her.

"I can't imagine how difficult this all must be for him. I should stop by. Bring one of my famous chicken potpies. I make it from scratch, you know." She angled her head and ran her fingers across her collarbone. "How does Friday sound?"

"Probably should check with Momma on that one." He'd do well to steer clear of the ranch that night, just in case.

"Sure, no problem." She fiddled with a pendant hanging from her necklace. "You and the boys still join your parents for dinners on Fridays?"

"Depends." Since his dad's accident, it seemed he spent more time over there than not. But Sally Jo didn't need to know that. She'd be liable to show up on his momma's doorstep and never leave. The poor girl really needed to find some other single guy to chase after.

"Where are you sitting?" She pivoted toward the bleachers and inched closer to him.

He stepped back. "Actually, I'm waiting on my folks." Now he wanted them to come more than ever. He faced the entrance and grinned to see his mom enter, pushing his dad in his chair. "If you'll excuse me…"

"Mind if I join you?" She pushed her lips out in what was probably supposed to be one of those CoverGirl pouty faces. "I hate sitting by myself."

Like she didn't know everyone in here. Then again, she'd stolen enough boyfriends to turn every female in Sage Creek against her. It would sure be nice if she set her sights on someone else, though.

"Sally Jo." His mom approached with her welcoming smile. "How nice to see you! How's your mother doing? I haven't talked with her since her surgery. Her knee holding up okay?"

Drake grimaced and fell into step with his mother as she and Sally Jo chatted it up. Was it too late to sit by Faith? He glanced about, to find her sandwiched between his sister and a bunch of her friends. She looked his way, her gaze sweeping from him to Sally Jo, then back to him with a raised eyebrow.

Did she think something was going on between him and Sally?

If so, did that bother her? At the thought, a smile tugged at his mouth.

Why did he care? He shouldn't. They were coworkers, and she was here on a short-term assignment. She was off-limits.

It'd be a lot easier to remember that if the woman wasn't so incredibly beautiful. And talented. And kind. And…off-limits.

After church, Faith found herself swept up in a group of laughing, talking women, most of whom were around her age. She stepped back, looking for an escape route, but Elizabeth grabbed her by the arm and tugged her to her side.

"Y'all, this is Faith Nichols. She's an artist from Austin, come to help Drake restore Trinity."

"Cool." The redhead grinned. "So, you're painting or what?"

Faith stood taller as all eyes, filled with admiration, shifted her way. She shook her head and explained her role.

"But she *is* quite the artist." Elizabeth hip-bumped her. "You should see some of her paintings." She shot Faith a mischievous smile. "I stalked your website."

"You have a website?" The girl with glasses

took out her phone. "I'd love to see it. What's it called?"

Faith told her and inched back into the circle. "It's mainly for commission work, though I do have a fair number of gallery pieces displayed." She looked up to find Drake watching her from across the room. A surge of heat flooded her cheeks, and she quickly averted her gaze.

She launched into a conversation on mixed media, to distract herself from the tall, muscular man who was developing a rather inconvenient pull on her.

Elizabeth's friends continued to fire questions and accolades at her as they perused her site on their phones, making her smile. At least some people in this town respected her artistic abilities.

Elizabeth tapped a knuckle against her chin. "You wouldn't happen to be free this weekend, would you?"

Other than horseback riding… Her pulse accelerated, and her gaze flew to Drake once again. He stood talking to a couple of his buddies. Feet shoulder distance apart, one hand resting on his shiny belt buckle, while the other rubbed his stubbled jaw.

Faith swallowed and focused back on Elizabeth. "I'm, uh… I've got some free time. Why?"

"A bunch of us will be working on the town

float. We could sure use an artist to help us out. Keep it from turning out hokey."

She looked from face to face, relaxing when smiles shone back at her. "When were you thinking?"

"We're meeting here Friday from 6:00 to 9:00 p.m., then again on Saturday, most likely from dawn until we finish. We'll all pitch in for pizza."

Faith chewed the inside of her lip. Might be smart to use the time to cut out some of the intricate glass pieces she needed for the restoration, or work on something for the Honey Locust. But she was tired of spending her evenings in a tiny hotel room with spotty internet and no cable.

The church had offered for Faith to stay with one of their members. Though that would've saved her a chunk of change, she'd vetoed the idea immediately. The last thing she needed was to have some high-and-mighty religious person watching her comings and goings.

But Elizabeth wasn't like that. She wasn't critical or judgmental and didn't quote Bible verses every time she spoke. Faith liked being around her. She reminded her of one of her few friends from college.

"Sure. I can do that." But she wasn't about to give up her horseback riding time. And that had nothing, zilch, nada to do with Drake. "Though I probably can't stay the whole time."

"Hey, we'll take whatever we can get." Elizabeth grinned.

"I'm not sure I'll have my car back by then." Apparently, the mechanic was waiting on some part.

"Not a problem." Elizabeth pulled a tube of lip balm from her pocket. "I'm sure you can catch a ride with Drake after work."

Stampeding ants invaded her gut. "I'd hate to put him out."

Elizabeth waved a hand. "He'll be heading this way anyway—he and some of his buddies volunteered to build the float. Having an extra body in his truck won't bother him none."

So Drake was going to be there. Meaning she'd be spending even more time with him. Every day at work. This weekend to help with the float. Then horseback riding.

She was doing a terrible job of distancing herself from him.

And unless she figured out a way to cool her emotional responses, she was heading straight for heartbreak.

Two weeks, three tops. She could do this. Finish the windows, hang out with some nice ladies on her off hours, then return home, never to see—or think about—Drake again.

Chapter Eleven

Drake pulled off his work gloves and wiped the sweat from his face. Only 10:00 a.m. and already near eighty degrees. A hard rain would feel mighty nice, but it would drench everything his guys had carted down from the attic. Then again, seeing how filthy everything was, a little drenching might be helpful.

He gazed at the pale blue sky, clear except for a handful of cotton ball clouds. No sign of rain that he could tell. Still, he'd be wise to buy some bins, get the church's overflow organized and put back. Once he finished all the repairs.

"How's it looking up there?"

He turned at Faith's voice. She wore fitted jean shorts and a purple tank top, and her long, chestnut hair was tied in a loose ponytail. Auburn highlights ran through the silky strands framing her face, and darker wisps rested on her delicate neck.

Since when did he pay attention to a woman's hair?

He took a swig of his water. "Honest answer? Worse than I'd expected. Those bats must've been roosting up there for some time. We had a leak and that, combined with the bat droppings, caused parts of the floor and drywall to rot."

"Wow. Sorry."

"We'll get 'er done. Oh, almost forgot. William made you something." He pulled a folded piece of paper from his back pocket and handed it over.

Her eyebrows shot up. As she opened the page, her face smoothed into the most radiant smile. "This is adorable. He made this for me?"

Drake nodded, captivated by the sparkle in her gray eyes—as if the colorful scribbles before her were a treasured piece of art. "Not sure what it's supposed to be, but…"

"Tell him I absolutely love it."

How was he supposed to maintain his distance from this woman when she looked at him like that? He gave a nervous cough. "I, uh, have to hit the hardware store this afternoon. Need anything?"

"Nope, but thanks."

The familiar rattle and hum of Lucy's twenty-some-year-old four door averted his attention. He and Faith strolled over to greet her as she parked and stepped out.

"Ma'am." He tipped his hat.

Lucy smiled. "Hi, Drake. Faith. I brought some boxes for you to go through. The ladies from my brunch club brought them over, for your historical search. I should have more come tomorrow evening, if not sooner. I sent out emails last night."

In other words, everyone and their long lost kin would be unloading their attics and basements.

She moved to her trunk and popped it open. "Drake, think you can help me with these? There's more in the backseat."

"No problem."

Faith eyed the loaded vehicle. "Wow. That's a lot of stuff."

Was she overwhelmed? Drake wondered. It wasn't right that the committee was pushing this job off on her. She had enough to manage with the windows. He should've said something at the meeting. Then again, her mention of the peeling paint had led to this whole mess. Besides, she seemed genuinely excited to dig through other people's junk.

He picked up a bulging box sealed with packing tape. "Want me to put this in the back of my pickup?"

"Sure." Faith followed with a smaller box, while Lucy, wearing a calf-length skirt that apparently made taking normal steps impossible, hobbled after them. "Did your team figure out what they want to do, if the murals aren't originals?"

Drake tensed. "Far's I'm concerned, the town doesn't need to spend the time or money changing something everyone's come to love for generations. There's history, then there's history."

Faith frowned, and he knew he'd spoken too harshly. But this wasn't something he cared to tiptoe around.

She crossed her arms. "It was a reasonable question."

"No sense pressing the matter. The committee'll let us know when—"

"You think you could stay longer?" Lucy clasped her hands in front of her. "If we need someone to paint the church's interior? I saw your work posted on your website. You're quite talented."

"I appreciate you saying that." Faith rubbed the back of her hand beneath her chin. "I'm not sure. I'd need to put in another bid."

Lucy waved a hand. "We can talk about that later. Once you go through all the old photographs and such. This won't be too much, will it?"

Drake swatted at a fly. "I'll help."

Faith looked at him with raised eyebrows. Was she surprised or upset? But he wanted to be there, to see what she found.

He needed to figure out how to get the committee off this historical registry business. Some things, like decades worth of memories, were more important.

Faith wiped dust from her hands. "You can help if you want."

He couldn't read her tone, and she didn't say much as they transferred the rest of the boxes. Nor did he. His thoughts were too jumbled. Was he holding too tight to the church, to how it looked? What if everyone pushed to change it?

He checked the time. "I best get going."

Faith gave a brisk nod, then started talking to Lucy about some type of art folks used in the nineteenth century. As if they were already planning to redo things.

If the committee had hired Leaded Pane like they were supposed to, they wouldn't be in this mess.

He huffed and got into his truck. The radio came on with the engine, a country tune. Not helping. He changed to Ag-Talk AM and let the host's nasally voice distract him.

Someone phoned in with a question on bloated heifers, prompting him to call his mom. His sister answered.

"How's everything going?"

She paused. "Same as usual. The boys are going stir-crazy, Dad's in a mood and Mom keeps disappearing into her office to do more number crunching."

"Can I talk to her?" He pulled into a parking spot in front of the hardware store.

"She's napping. Said she didn't sleep much last night. Did you get a chance to talk to Jason yet?"

He rubbed a hand over his face. "You know what selling that place will do to Mom. To both of them."

"I'm not sure what else we can do. The bills keep coming, and Dad's got a lot more doctor visits ahead."

"I'll stop by the bank later this week. See if Jason has a few minutes."

He ended the call and walked into the hardware store. A gust of cold air swept over him, carrying with it the scent of metal mixed with cedar and pine, on account of all the air fresheners Clint's wife plugged in every outlet. That and her need to place knickknacks and fake flowers all over the place made no sense to him.

Two of his buddies stood talking at the counter, a large sheet of paper unrolled between them.

"Hey, there." Drake sauntered over and shook their hands. "How're things?"

"Great." Neil, his old football buddy, grinned. "I was telling Clint here about my plans to build an outdoor obstacle course and training center."

"A what?"

"You know, those big adult jungle gym type contraptions, like you see on TV."

"Interesting." Drake studied his friend's sketch. "Did you mention all this to the folks at city hall?"

"Yep. They think it might help bring some revenue in. Now I just need to figure out where to put the thing. And who to have build it." He offered a crooked smile.

"Call me in a month or so, once I get this restoration off my plate."

He left the men to talk sports, tourism and reality television, and headed toward the lumberyard out back.

Unfortunately, he'd forgotten about all the boxes in the bed of his pickup and had to do some finagling to situate his building supplies so they wouldn't go flying out.

Back at the church, he balanced a drywall sheet on his shoulders and headed inside, nearly colliding with Faith as she was coming out.

She sprang back. "Excuse me."

"My fault. I need to pay better attention to where I'm going." He smiled. "I'm liable to knock a person out with this thing."

Her frown suggested she was still irritated with him. And just when they'd started to get along.

Though he had to admit, she looked mighty cute mad. "About earlier… I didn't mean to get under your skin. I know you're trying to do the right thing."

She studied him. "Thanks." She offered a slight smile, one that could easily undo him, if he wasn't careful.

On second thought, maybe it'd be safer, emotionally speaking, to keep her angry.

Faith returned to her work area, casting one last glance over her shoulder. Whenever Drake was around, whenever he turned his blue eyes on her, her breath hitched. She'd never reacted to men that way.

Except Josh, and look how that turned out.

She didn't come here to get tangled up in some summer romance. She came to do a job, get some press coverage, then go home.

If only her heart would cooperate.

A gust of wind swept her loose hair into her face, a few strands catching on her eyelashes. Readjusting her ponytail, she crossed the lawn to her light table, where she'd started to repair a bent window. But first she had to plug in a heating pad she needed to place on the panel.

She grabbed the end of her second extension cord, the first being utilized for her light box, and headed back to the church.

It wasn't long enough to reach the entrance, leaving a fifty-foot gap. With a huff, she dropped it on the ground and glanced about. One of Drake's crew had to have an extra cord she could borrow.

"What's up?" Drake's deep voice caught her off guard.

She inhaled to regain her emotional center, faced him and explained her problem. "You wouldn't happen to have one I could borrow, would you?"

In the middle of cutting a piece of drywall, he set his utility knife aside, dusted off his hands and straightened. "Sure. I can get you one."

"Thanks." She leaned against the side of the church and scrolled through her Facebook notifications while she waited for him to return.

Drake stepped out of the church with a bundle of orange cord. "Will this work?"

She replaced her phone in her pocket. "It should." Her cell chimed an incoming call. "Excuse me." She glanced at the number on her screen. It was the repair shop. "Hello, this is Faith."

"Howdy, Ms. Nichols. This is Mike from Mike's Auto Body. Your little gem's finished and ready to go."

"Great! I can pick it up this evening."

"Actually, think you can get down here before three? Or maybe tomorrow morning? I promised the missus I'd leave early today so I could take care of some stuff on the home front."

"Uh…sure. No problem. Thanks, Mike." No more relying on Drake for rides.

She frowned. That fact bothered her more than it should have.

"If I were to wager a guess, I'd say you've received a piece of good news." He shot her his adorable lopsided grin.

She nodded and relayed her conversation.

"I'll drive you down there."

"Oh, no. There's no need for that. I'll ride my bike over."

"Don't be ridiculous. That'll add at least twenty minutes both ways. In the late afternoon heat. Going uphill there and back. Barefoot." He winked, causing her stomach to do a rather annoying flip.

"I wouldn't mind heading into town, anyway." He tossed a scrap of drywall into a nearby wheelbarrow. "I could sure use an ice-cold Coke. Or maybe a Slurpee. Hawaiian Punch. No, blue raspberry."

The mention of fruit flavors reminded her of his chubby-cheeked boys emerging from the convenience store sucking on candy bigger than their mouths. Ten minutes later, sticky pink and blue had stained their faces, teeth and tongues.

He lifted his Stetson and swiped his forehead with a towel. "You ready to leave now?"

She'd look like an idiot, or unreasonably stubborn, if she refused. Besides, it was just a ride.

"Um…" She felt like an awkward middle

schooler being asked to a dance. "Yeah. Just let me grab my purse."

Drake beat her to his truck and stood with the passenger door open.

Her face heated when his blue eyes met hers. "Thanks." She slid in, her arm brushing his and sending a jolt of electricity through her.

"Should've been more gentlemanly from the get-go." A hint of pink colored his cheeks. Probably from working in the heat all day. "Maybe then we would've started off on a better foot."

"Better than a car wreck?" She quirked an eyebrow at him.

"Ah, come on now." He rested a hand on the top of her door, his strong frame only inches from her, so close she could smell his minty breath. "You going to hold that against me forever?" Mirth crinkled the skin around his eyes.

"Something like that." Her pulse drummed in her ears. "Though I suppose, now that my car's fixed, I should let it go."

His expression sobered. His mouth parted, as if he wanted to say something, but then he slapped the top of his truck, closed her door and rounded to the driver's side. The cab filled with the scents of leather and sawdust as he slid behind the wheel.

As usual, his radio came on when he started the engine. "I s'pose I should let you choose the station, huh?"

"You don't have to."

He eased down the gravel road. "The way your nose wrinkles every time Hank Williams comes on, I beg to differ." His wink stalled her breath.

He probably had all the Sage Creek ladies chasing after him.

Only she'd never seen him flirt with any, not that she'd been around him much outside of work. Except at church. And the picnic. Both times he'd been a doting father and son. What was it the preacher had said last Wednesday, about families holding tight through the good and the hard?

Something her parents, clearly, had been unable to do. Why was Drake's family so different than hers had been?

She slid him a sideways glance, watched as he continued to fiddle with the radio, going from static to hip-hop, then classical.

After a few minutes, he turned it off. "That's a sign, you know?"

"What's that?"

"The fact that I can't find your station."

"Oh, yeah?"

He nodded. "It means…" He chuckled and shook his head. "I got nothing. Apparently, I'm plumb out of funny comebacks today."

She laughed. "Least you're honest." She was learning there was a great deal of truth in that statement. Honest, hardworking, loyal, based on how he treated his boys and family.

And out of her reach, by about one hundred miles, to be exact.

As they neared Wilma's Kitchen, the rich aroma of fried chicken and roasting garlic caused Faith's stomach to growl loudly.

Heat climbed her neck, and she pressed her fingertips to her mouth. "Excuse me."

"Mite hungry, are we?"

"Maybe a little."

"I could eat something myself."

"I thought you wanted a Slurpee."

"An iced Coke and bacon cheeseburger will do." He eased into a slanted parking spot. "You mind?"

"What?"

"If we stop for a bite. Long as we're here and all."

"For lunch?" Her limbs felt jittery. This was quickly turning into more than a ride—a thought her rebellious heart found much too appealing.

That was precisely why she needed to decline. But she couldn't really say no; he was the one driving, after all. And she was starved.

She offered what she hoped appeared a casual smile. "Sure."

Two hungry coworkers eating together. Nothing more.

Right?

Regardless, in less than a month, she'd be back in Austin, pursuing her dream career, with this handsome cowboy long forgotten.

Chapter Twelve

"After you." Drake held the diner door open for Faith and breathed in the rich aromas of fresh baked apple pie and burned coffee.

"Thank you." She hurried inside and he followed, stopping at the Seat Yourself sign to glance about. His gaze shot to Faith. Her eyes, gray and rimmed with green, captivated him.

She quickly looked away. Heads turned in their direction. His old football coach, sitting with the high school math teacher, raised an eyebrow. His smirk made Drake tense.

"Drake, good to see you." Sally Jo approached in her waitressing uniform, her voice two notches too sweet. She wore gold glitter eye shadow and penguin earrings, her mousy hair pulled back in a crocheted headband. "You haven't come in for a spell. I was starting to think maybe you quit eating."

"Just been busy, is all." He'd liked this place a whole lot better when Sally's grandmother ran it.

"Well, don't make a habit of it." She placed a manicured hand on her cocked hip. "Folks might get to worrying."

He touched Faith's elbow, finding her skin soft and cool, and motioned with his head toward an empty booth along the far wall. "Over there look okay?"

She glanced about, looking like a newborn calf caught in a bull pen. Not that he blamed her, with how folks were staring at them. Some people had too much time on their hands.

According to his sister, a group of church ladies had even taken to praying for Drake and his "situation," more than ever since Faith had arrived in town. They were certain his boys needed a momma.

He was inclined to agree, but one couldn't jump into those kinds of relationships. That would hurt the boys far more than it'd help them. That was reason enough not to strike up a romance with an out-of-towner.

No matter how beautiful, tenderhearted or talented.

Heads nodded in greeting as they passed. He removed his Stetson and placed it on a hook near the bathroom, then joined Faith at the table.

"This place has the best grilled cheese around."

He pulled a menu from between the wall and condiments and handed it over.

"Thanks. I guess this is one of those places where everyone knows your name."

"I 'spect all of Sage Creek would fit that description."

"I've noticed."

Was that a bad thing? Her blank expression gave no indication. "How you liking the town so far?"

"Haven't seen much of it, except in passing." She focused on her menu, leaving Drake to rack his brain for another conversation starter. Strange that he was having such a hard time pulling the girl out of her shell. She wasn't like the women he was used to, who batted their eyelashes and giggled whenever a man happened by.

She reminded him of Lydia. Man, had she been something. Aloof at first, then swinging from friendly to stubborn faster than a swaybacked mule after a feeding. But Lydia had never felt the need to prove herself, not like Faith seemed to.

Then again, he'd never questioned his wife's capabilities like he had Faith's. He winced inwardly, remembering the look on her face when she'd overheard his two less-than-favorable conversations.

Sally Jo glided over with water glasses. "Let me guess. Bacon cheeseburger, extra cheese and mayo, with fries and a double order of coleslaw."

She gave him a smile that was probably meant to be demure, but reminded him of a duck's bill. Her expression tightened as her gaze shifted to Faith.

"You ready?" he asked Faith.

She nodded. "I'll take the Italian sub with a side salad."

Sally made notes on her order pad, then inched closer to Drake. "Your regular?"

He gave a one-shoulder shrug. "Why not? With a Coke."

"You got it." Her smiled widened, revealing a smudge of pink lipstick on her front tooth, and she held his gaze for a second longer than was comfortable. She was really laying it on this afternoon.

He resisted the urge to fidget, and instead looked at Faith and took a slow drink of water.

She raised an eyebrow, the upturned corners of her mouth indicating she found this little interchange quite amusing.

Luckily, before things became too awkward, an older gentlemen two tables down called for a coffee refill.

Sally released a sigh. "Coming." She flashed Drake one of her less than winning smiles. "Catch you in a few."

"That was interesting." Faith pulled out a neon-green pill organizer and popped open the first compartment. She poured four different colored pills—vitamins?—into her hand. "How long has she been pining for you?"

He coughed. "Uh… Her grandmother opened this place some thirty years ago, after her husband died. Her daughter, Sally's momma, ran it for a while, but now she pretty much stays in the office."

"That didn't answer my question."

He gave a nervous chuckle. "Sixth grade. Mr. Holman's PE class." Back when he'd been a scrawny, four-foot-five, ninety-pound kid just learning to catch a football.

"You've lived here all your life?"

"Born and raised, except for a short stint in College Station, where I went to college. Same for my parents before me, and their parents before them. Matter of fact, all of us got baptized and married at Trinity Faith."

"Wow, that's a lot of history."

"What about you? How long have you lived in Austin?"

"Going on ten years."

"You like it?"

"Most of the time." She smiled. "It's got a great art community. And amazing food."

"Your folks live nearby?"

She visibly tensed. "Nope. My mom's got a studio apartment in Missouri, and my dad's living large in northern New York, about as far from my mom as he can get."

"Sorry to hear that."

She flicked a hand. "It's not a big deal. They divorced a long time ago. When I was eight, though religion killed any love between them long before that."

Clearly, he'd hit a nerve. Best thing to do would be to leave it alone, except she'd been entrusted with an important, historically significant job. If she had a thing against religion, the committee would want to know.

He moved his water aside. "What does that mean?"

Her gaze remained fixed on his, though it softened some. "My mom found her faith," she said, "and not long after that, the fighting started. Three years later, almost to the day, the divorce was finalized."

How was he supposed to respond to that? "That must've been rough."

"It happens. Though I've always wondered how things might've turned out if my mom had found something else to occupy her time. Like crochet. Or quilting."

"I take it you're not a fan of church, then?"

She stared at him for an extended moment. "Whatever people need to get them through. So long as they don't slam me with Bible verses."

"I see." Not only did she live almost two hours away and was fixing to leave as soon as they finished the restoration, but she was against what mattered most to him—his faith. The two of them were incompatible in the most significant ways.

He wasn't sure what bothered him more—the barriers between them or the emotional sting that truth brought.

Faith dropped her crumpled napkin onto her plate. She'd clearly offended Drake. What kind of idiot started talking smack about another person's faith? Although it was the truth. Mom had started going to church, then began pestering Dad to go with her, to quit swearing and drinking, and a slew of other things.

They soon got so caught up in arguing they forgot about Faith entirely. Until after the divorce; then she became their pawn. Their assets had long since been divided, and in her mom's case, spent. Yet they still used Faith to hurt and manipulate each other.

Sally Jo sashayed over, her gaze lingering on Faith before shifting to Drake. "Can I get you anything else? A slice of fresh baked apple pie?"

He glanced at Faith and she shook her head.

"We're good." He paid and led the way out to his truck, pausing, as usual, to hold the door for her.

"Thanks."

He gave a quick nod, his eyes searching hers, as if mentally sifting through words, or maybe he was trying to figure her out. Because in his world, everyone went to church, got married at nineteen, had two or three kids, and spent Sunday nights gathered around a family dinner table?

So why did the religion, the whole faith and family thing, work for people like Drake and not her?

She climbed into the passenger's seat, ignoring Drake's outstretched hand.

His touch—even a simple look from him—was beginning to prove dangerous.

"Looks like it's going to rain." He gazed toward storm clouds steadily approaching. "Probably should call the guys, have them bring in all those bins I lugged down from the attic."

She nodded. Good thing she'd sealed all the church windows with plastic.

She had, hadn't she?

He eyed her one last time, his expression unreadable, then closed her door and rounded the truck to the driver's side.

Initially, their conversation felt stilted as they drove to the auto mechanic. But as he shared stories of storms he'd been caught in, most of them when he was a kid, she began to relax. He seemed to, as well.

"Then there was that year at the Stock and Steed Rodeo." He chuckled. "It was my first time goat tying."

She raised an eyebrow.

"You never heard of it?"

"No."

"Stick around long enough, I'll take you to see one." He winked, and her face heated. "I was pretty cocky. Figured I'd show all the other kids in my division how it was done. I went out on my horse full throttle, jumped down and took after the little critter. I got tangled in the rope, and splat, landed face-first in the mud."

She laughed.

"Must've been at least three inches thick, and I sank deep. Lost my man card for sure. Took me years, and some intense steer wrestling—"

"That's a thing?"

"Haven't you been to a rodeo or state fair? Never joined the 4-H?"

"Nope."

He shook his head like she'd somehow missed out, not having seen a bunch of dirty, sweaty men tackle bulls. Funny how she'd thought the same thing, a couple days ago, when he said he'd never been to Austin.

He pulled into a lot shared by a small grocery store and Mike's auto repair shop. A blue pickup with a dented fender and peeling paint was parked in the shade of a large oak.

Drake parked up by the shop's entrance and cut the engine. "Bet you'll be glad to get your wheels back."

"Definitely." She reached for her door.

He touched her arm, sending a jolt of electricity through her. "I know I've said this already, but I'm mighty sorry for all this trouble. And... well, everything."

"No problem." Hopefully that meant he regretted all the stuff he'd said about her to his friend. And Lucy.

Faith grabbed her purse and got out, then beat him inside. The place was empty except for a yellow-tinged computer that had to be at least fifteen years old, and a rotary phone. And an old-fashioned black Rolodex.

A tall, lanky man—Mike, according to his name tag—met her at the counter. "You must be Faith."

She nodded.

"Your little jewel's all spiffed up and ready to go." He handed her the receipt. "I took the liberty of washing her up all nice and pretty for you."

"Thanks. So we're good, then? Everything's covered?"

"Yeah. My buddy's insurance took care of it."

She glanced at Drake, to find him lingering near a tire display, watching her. When they made eye contact, he adjusted his hat and averted his gaze.

"You're good to go." Mike flashed a grin, revealing a mouthful of crooked, yellow teeth. "I'll drive her around for you."

"Thanks, Mike."

He gave a brisk nod and disappeared back into his shop.

Drake strode to the door and held it open. "Guess you don't need me anymore."

Though he offered a playful smile, his gaze held hers a moment too long.

As if he was disappointed he'd no longer be driving her around. She hated to admit that she felt the same, which was crazy, considering how much they butted heads.

Her phone dinged an incoming email. She swiped her finger across the screen and stopped in midstep. Jeremy Pratt, from *Lone Star Gems*.

Hopefully with good news. She pulled it up.

Good afternoon, Ms. Nichols,
I trust all is well. I spoke with my editor; though he has not completely nixed the idea of running a feature on you and your church project, he did express some hesitation. It would be incredibly helpful if you could take pictures as you go, preferably within the next few days, then email them to me. I'll keep you updated and will let you know if I need anything else.
Jeremy

Great. Just when things were beginning to look up. Without that magazine write-up, her time here would be a waste. She'd barely make enough, after paying for supplies and travel expenses, to cover her electric bill.

Each day, she seemed to be proving her father right.

That was something she refused to do. If the feature fell through, if the restoration project turned into a bust, she'd simply find a plan B. Like creating a phenomenal series for the Honey Locust. For now, she'd do whatever necessary to finish her job *and* get a feature, maybe even front cover of *Lone Star Gems* magazine.

Chapter Thirteen

That evening, Drake pulled into the parking lot and scanned the handful of cars gathered near the entrance. Faith's wasn't among them. Maybe he should stay out here, wait for her. Except it looked like his sister was already doing that.

She'd brought his boys as he'd asked.

William was hanging over the bike rack, his feet in the air, head dangling maybe two feet from the ground, while Trevor jumped off the stairs. It looked like he was trying to see how far he could go. The boy wasn't doing too badly, the little athlete.

Drake stepped out of his truck and sauntered over to his youngest. He surprised him with a tickle to the ribs. "Hey there, big fella."

William giggled and landed on his feet. "Daddy!" He barreled into Drake's legs and snagged him in a two-arm hold. "Where's Ms. Faith?"

An image of her in the truck, encouraging the

boys as they drew, that sweet smile lifting her cheekbones, filled his mind, stalling his movement. "She's coming, but she won't have time to play."

"Aw." William's bottom lip poked out.

With a laugh, Drake plucked his little guy off the ground and tossed him over his shoulder, then greeted his oldest. "What do you say, Trevman. You have a good day?"

"Grandma let me name a new calf."

"Did she now?"

He nodded. "She said maybe I could tend to her and enter her in the fair."

Drake smiled. That's what he liked to hear—that his boys were learning to be men, and not staring at a television screen all day. "I bet you'd be real good at that." He pulled him into a headlock hug.

Trevor grinned and raced back up the stairs, soon preparing for another jump.

Drake sauntered over to his sister, set William on his feet and gave her a one-arm hug. "Thanks for bringing the boys."

"No problem." She shaded her eyes and shifted toward the street. "Faith still coming?"

"Yep. She was working on something when I left. Said she wanted to finish up and would meet us later."

"Good. Oh. Here she comes now."

He turned, a strange, jittery feeling sweeping through him. Faith pulled in and parked on the far side of his truck. She'd tied her hair back like she often did, with wavy strands framing her face.

His littlest ran to meet her as she stepped from her car, holding a saggy floral backpack.

"Hey, little guy." She dropped to one knee and gave William a sideways hug.

Trevor soon joined them, standing a few feet away, his lips twitching as if reining in a smile.

Elizabeth hip-bumped Drake. "They sure took to Faith, huh?"

A lump lodged in his throat. "Looks that way." The more time they spent with her, the more attached they'd become, and the more heartbroken they'd be when she left.

He cleared his throat, stepped closer and tipped his hat.

A tinge of pink colored her cheeks. "Hi."

"Hey, girl!" Elizabeth called out while bounding toward her. "You have no idea how glad we are to have you. A real artist. Branchville's got nothing on us this year."

"Who?" Faith rubbed her collarbone. She'd changed from the powder blue T-shirt she'd worn at work to a sheer, ruffled blouse over a pink undershirt.

"A town not far from here," Elizabeth said. "The parade's a county affair. It brings folks from all over. The winning float gets mentioned in the paper and the winners get a trophy that's probably made of plastic but gets displayed with pride."

"And bragging rights for a year." Drake grinned.

A hot breeze swept over him. He glanced at his jeans, covered in a layer of grime and sawdust, and the sweat marks darkening his shirt. He had a spare in his truck. He'd be smart to change before heading in.

"Excuse me. I'll meet y'all inside in a few." Before heading for the truck, he made eye contact with each of his boys in turn. "You two, go with your aunt Elizabeth. And do what she says, you hear?"

"And Miss Faith?" William piped up.

He caught her gaze, and she blushed and looked away. He nodded. "And Miss Faith."

He opened his truck door and rummaged through an old duffel bag tucked behind the driver's seat. Unfortunately, his spare shirt, a faded tractor-pull T, wasn't much better than what he had on. Bright yellow with red lettering, it would make him look like a striped canary. Worse, it was about half a size too small. It had been sitting in his truck, wadded up, since the day he got it.

Which shirt would be better—the one that he'd worked in all day, or the one that could blind people if they looked at it too long?

An image of Faith with her delicate eyebrows

raised, her rosy lips curved in a slight smirk, came to mind, heating his cheeks.

He shouldn't care what she thought of him. There was no way anything would ever work out between the two of them. Even if she weren't completely opposed to his faith, she wouldn't be around much longer.

Then again, maybe that was what this was about. Maybe it was Faith's unavailability that drew him to her, sort of like the forbidden fruit. If so, his feelings toward her would fade soon enough.

He traded his sweaty T-shirt for the canary-like one and climbed the school's steps. His phone rang. He glanced at the screen. Pearson. Dad hadn't been out of the hospital a month, and already the vultures gathered.

"You need something?" He opened the doors to a gust of air-conditioning.

"How're you doing?"

"Holding my own."

"And your folks? They're managing all right? Such a shame about the accident. Must be hard to see—"

"Quit circling the hay barn. We both know why you're calling, and we also know you aren't aiming to offer a fair price."

"If you'd hear me out, I'm confident you'll find my offer quite reasonable."

"Doesn't matter what I think. My mom already told you how she felt."

"Yes, but that was before…" He gave a melo-dramatic sigh. "I thought perhaps she'd had more time to think, now that she and your dad have gotten more settled into their new routine. And, well, not to be insensitive, but I suspect the hospital bills have begun to trickle in."

"You snake. Trying to profit from a man's misfortune." He paused outside the gym and watched everyone through the door's window. His boys were climbing up and down a set of roll-away bleachers while Faith, Elizabeth and half a dozen other Trinity Faith folks leaned over a long sheet of butcher paper. Probably looking at float sketches.

"Now, Drake, you know me better than that."

He gave a harsh chuckle. "That's the first bit of truth I've heard you say. I do know you, Pearson. I know you real well. So unless you're calling to see about lending a hand out at the ranch—"

"All I'm asking is that you talk to your mother. Help her see the wisdom—"

"Goodbye." He ended the call and released a heavy breath. Truth be told, Drake's folks were running out of options. Unless he figured something out soon, they'd be forced to sell. But not to a belly crawler like Pearson.

Faith glanced up as Drake entered, and her gaze snagged on his. But then she caught a glimpse of his shirt. A snicker burst out, which she quickly covered with a cough, then another until her mirth subsided.

The only way that would happen was if she didn't look his way. That cowboy was something else. All manly with his leather boots, faded jeans…and bright yellow T-shirt with a cartoonish tractor in a red circle. Bold letters arched above this: Pull 'Em Like a Man. The hem of his shirt barely hit his waistband and the neck looked snug enough to nearly strangle the guy.

Just thinking about it prodded a giggle, and made her feel exponentially less awkward.

Elizabeth glanced up. "Drake, come—" She pulled her lips in over her teeth, laughter dancing in her eyes.

Making it absolutely impossible for Faith to hold hers. "If you'll excuse me." She dashed to a drinking fountain on the far wall, chuckling as soon as her back was turned. She stayed at the fountain, taking small enough sips to keep from choking, until certain she could return composed.

Rejoining the group, she found Drake standing over the trailer one of the guys had brought, which supposedly they would cover in plywood. He shot Faith a glance, and his neck turned blotchy red.

Almost initiating another fit of laughter.

"So…" Elizabeth's mouth continued to twitch. "…how about you big, burly men work on the float platform while we ladies plan out the overall design?"

"Sure. Yeah, whatever."

Faith quirked an eyebrow at him; it sounded like he'd intentionally deepened his voice with that response. And he seemed to be doing some sort of chest-puffed, shoulders-broadened body builder's stance. Poor guy. Trying to regain the last shred of his dignity.

It was strange, and disconcerting, that she found this side of Drake all the more endearing.

"I say we divide the float in half." A girl with short blond hair drew a line across the illustration Elizabeth had sketched on butcher paper. "The front could be an old Western jail. You know, with rustic wooden siding and a thick overhang." She started to tap on the screen of her phone.

"That sounds like an awful lot of work." An older lady to Faith's right scrunched her nose. "We don't have much time. I thought we'd do something simple. Maybe some PVC pipes for the bars and chicken wire or something wrapped around them."

"Chicken wire?" One of guys helping Drake snorted. "This isn't a rooster roundup, Anna Jane."

"Mock if you want, but I'd rather have a simple float than an unfinished one."

"What if…" Faith grabbed her sketchbook and pencil bag from her backpack and flipped to an unused page. She pulled out a charcoal pencil and chanced a quick glance at Drake.

Shrunken shirt or not, he looked incredibly handsome, down on one knee, hammering nails into plywood. When he rose to grab a nail from a bucket to his right, she quickly averted her gaze.

She tapped her pencil against her chin. "We could do more of a cartoon-style jail, like they have at Disney."

"Never been," Anna Jane said.

"I'll Google it." A lanky teen with a long, thin neck strolled over. Slouching, he started tapping on his phone screen.

Faith drew jail bars set in a building made from stone. "Like this." She sketched two center bars bent away from one another, as if someone had tried to pry them apart. Then she used a mixture of block and bubble letters to sketch the word *jail* above them.

"Ah." Elizabeth nodded. "That might work. And shouldn't take much time."

"Or—" Faith flipped the page and started to draw again "—we could keep the old Western jail idea but make the outside look like plaster or concrete instead of wood. Then all we'd need to do is cut the basic shape from plywood and paint it, using plaster to create a rough texture. We could still use the PVC pipes on the side, painted black, for the actual cell portion."

"Love it!" Elizabeth squeezed Faith's hand. "See why we wanted you here?"

Anna Jane watched over Faith's shoulder as she continued to sketch out her idea. "Not a bad plan. Supplies shouldn't cost much, either." She angled her head. "Is there anything you can't do?"

Faith gave a quick laugh. "What?"

"You restore windows, paint, make beautiful glass jewelry and mosaics." Anna Jane smiled. "Elizabeth was talking you up before you arrived."

All eyes turned to Faith, including Drake's.

"Oh. Well, thank you." It felt good, and awkward, to be appreciated. Dropping her gaze, she returned to her sketch, adding wheels, an outline of the road and wisps of grass.

"What's your website?" The slouchy kid crossed one arm over his chest, phone still raised.

Elizabeth rattled it off with a grin. "She's got some good stuff. I'm telling you. High quality."

Anna Jane pushed herself to her feet with a hand on the small of her back. "How much for a pair of earrings? My mom's birthday's coming up and I'd sure love to get her something pretty. From a bona fide artist. Could you sign them?"

Faith wrinkled her brow. "The earrings?"

"No." Anna Jane waved a hand. "That cardboard thing they come attached to."

"Uh…sure. If you want." She'd never been asked that before, or been treated like this. Like she was famous or something.

"One of these days you should do a painting party." Elizabeth poked through the paintbrushes that had spilled from Faith's backpack. "Like they do in the city."

A teen with carrot-toned hair squealed. "I've been to one of those. They're so much fun."

"We'd pay you, of course." Elizabeth shoulder-bumped her.

"I'd be all over that."

"Same."

Faith's smile grew as the girls all around her shared their enthusiasm for the event. The money would be awesome, but a night with friends… Were these women friends?

They were becoming so, Elizabeth especially. Never in her strangest dreams would Faith have thought she'd feel so comfortable around church people.

Her phone chimed. It was a text from her client—her only client—back in Austin. Finally. Hopefully, she was contacting Faith to tell her she approved of the preliminary sketches she'd sent over a month ago, and was ready to mail her deposit.

Faith pulled up the message: Problem. Call me.

Her chest tightened. Not now. She didn't need any more setbacks. But hopefully, it was minor. Hadn't everyone told her this woman was high maintenance?

And with a pocketbook to match.

"Excuse me." She stood and walked out of earshot before dialing Mrs. Hamlin's number.

The woman answered on the first ring. "That good-for-nothing ex-husband of mine is obsessed with ruining my life. But if he thinks I'm going to roll over and play doormat, he's got another think coming."

"What's this about?"

"What did I ever see in that man? Draining my account—mine! How he found out about it in the first place is beyond me. It had to have been my mother. She's always—"

"Your account?" Faith swallowed, feeling like she was about to get sick. "What do you mean? What account?"

"The only one that hasn't been frozen. I opened it a few years ago."

"What're you saying?"

"Thanks to that low-life ex-husband of mine, that floor-to-ceiling mural I've been planning on for over a decade is out of the question now."

She went on to talk about how long she'd been dreaming about the project and what it meant to her, but Faith barely listened. All she could think about was the loss of income—money she desperately needed.

Leaning back against the wall, she closed her eyes and pinched the bridge of her nose. Then she took a deep breath and mustered all the professionalism she possessed. "I'm really sorry to hear this. I know you're terribly disappointed."

This triggered more ranting, to which Faith offered her best platitudes before hanging up and returning to the others.

The teen with shaggy hair stood to meet her. "What'd you say your name was?"

"Faith Nichols."

"From Austin, right?"

She tensed at his curt tone. "Yeah."

"Is your dad that professor who wrote the book on atheism?"

"Uh, yeah. Why?"

He stepped closer. "I'm reading an interview you did a couple years ago where you said, 'Why are people so concerned about what my father does or doesn't believe? If his logic concerns them, then their beliefs must not be all that strong.'"

The teen with the carrot-colored hair looked at Faith with big, droopy eyes. "You don't believe in God?"

"I didn't say—"

Elizabeth stood and crossed her arms. "What's this about, Jacob? Someone step on your toes? Give you the wrong end of a paintbrush?"

His frown deepened. "Seems to me folks would want someone with a respect for Trinity Faith to be working on them windows."

Faith rubbed her arm. "I have a great deal of

respect for the church and its history. I've spent hours—"

"Hold up." Drake's firm voice silenced everyone. He shot Jacob a stern look. "You need to chill before I toss you out of here. Here's the deal." He swept his gaze from face to face. "She was hired on for one reason and one reason only. Because she was the best woman for the job."

He slid a scowl back to the kid. "You got a problem with that, I suggest you take it up with Lucy and her team."

Faith stared at her sketch pad, tears burning her eyes. She started to gather her things.

"Wait, Faith." Elizabeth reached out and touched her hand. "Don't go. Jacob's just being a jerk."

The teen to her right threw an eraser at him.

"We're glad you're here." Anna Jane patted Faith's shoulder.

Her gaze bounced to Drake, and he gave her that crooked smile that always turned her insides to jelly.

"So am I," he said.

A rush of warmth swept through her, triggering a smile that she almost let loose.

He'd stood up for her, and that meant a lot.

Too much.

Chapter Fourteen

Drake gathered his tools and corralled his boys. Halfway to the door, Trevor paused in a lunge position, arms bent, hands fisted. "Race you to the truck. On the count of three."

William lifted his chin, brow pinched, then took off.

"Not fair! You cheated!" Trevor raced after him, catching the tyke at the door.

Drake chuckled and cast one last glance back at Faith. She stood surrounded by the other ladies, flipping through her sketchbook. Apparently, she'd awakened their inner artists.

While cleaning up, they'd spent the better part of the last fifteen minutes talking about painting parties and such. And of course, Elizabeth, being the dreamer and plotter that she was, suggested Faith could turn the parties into a business, should she stick around once the restoration concluded.

Something Faith clearly wasn't planning on doing, though she had given his sister a cute little head tilt.

Almost as if she were considering the idea. What if she chose to stay?

Such speculation wasn't helping him maintain an appropriate emotional distance. Tossing all thoughts of Faith aside, he met his boys at the large double doors leading to the parking lot, where he knew they'd be.

Between the heavy metal and the rusted hinges, neither was strong enough to push their way outside. Not for lack of trying, though. With the way Trevor was ramming the bar with his shoulder, the boy would be black-and-blue come sundown.

Apparently William had given up, because he sat on the floor, pouting.

"Got you trapped, huh?" Drake winked at his oldest, then scooped his youngest up, tickling his crabby mood out of him. Once outside, Trevor ran straight for the bike rack, his favorite makeshift jungle gym, and William started whining and squirming to get down.

"Nope." Drake grabbed his oldest by the elbow and guided him toward the truck. "Grandma's got dinner waiting." He hit Unlock on his key fob and deposited William on his feet. The little one started to dart away, but Drake hooked him by the waist and plopped him into his car seat.

"Here." He handed him his favorite plastic dinosaur to keep him occupied. Then, as Trevor climbed in, Drake rounded the vehicle and slid behind the wheel.

By the time he hit Main Street, both boys were belting out the chorus to one of their favorite songs. They sure loved music, just like their momma. Man, that girl had liked to sing.

He thought of Faith and her heavy metal and chuckled. She'd bring a whole different kind of singing to their world, that's for sure.

If only she lived closer. And shared his faith.

Why did she keep invading his thoughts?

As he neared his folks' place, he thought of his mother's southern cooking, and his stomach rumbled. Faith would love Momma's buttermilk biscuits. Hopefully, she'd made one of her famous desserts, too. Like rhubarb pie or maybe oatmeal raisin cookies.

His mom greeted them on the porch wearing her favorite floral apron over a pair of loose jeans. The boys started clamoring to get out of the truck, calling for Meemaw the minute he parked.

Once freed, they raced toward her, Trevor asking more questions than a person could process, while William talked about the float.

"Momma." Drake greeted her with a kiss to the cheek. "You have a good day?"

"Wouldn't have it any other way." Her tense

expression said otherwise. She shielded her eyes and gazed out toward the cows in the pasture. "Had another calf born today. Dillon saw to it before he left. He said both momma and baby are doing well."

"Good. How's Dad?"

"Hungry, and anxious for a big ol' slice of my home-baked peach cobbler."

Drake grinned. "With ice cream?"

"Of course." A genuine smile softened the worry lines in her face. "After all, it's not every day my boy brings a girl home."

He choked on his saliva. "Momma, you got to stop talking like that. You're the one who invited her over."

"Don't you just love how God works?" She patted the side of his face, then turned to the boys. "We've got some brand-new baby calves. Want to meet them?"

"Yeah!" the boys said in unison.

She looked at Drake. "That all right with you? Won't take but a minute. Dad's watching *Judge Judy*, and dinner's simmering on the stove."

"No problem."

"Thanks." She started to walk toward the barn, then stopped. "Biscuits are in the oven. Can you pull them out when the timer rings?"

"Will do." He glanced down the dirt road, where the dust had already settled. The girls would be arriving any minute. Faith, joining them for dinner. Jittery energy, kind of like he used to get before having to give speeches back in high school, surged through him.

Hopefully, Mom would behave and keep her knowing smiles—and her matchmaking goals— to herself. Still, it was nice to see her happy.

He turned toward the house. The wooden plank he'd laid atop the stairs in a makeshift wheelchair ramp bowed beneath him. He needed to make something more permanent, as soon as he got time. There were a lot of repairs and re-models he needed to tackle, but his to-do list always seemed to stretch past the available hours in a day.

What would it be like to have someone to help on the home front, someone sweet and funny and smart?

The more he entertained such thoughts, the more miserable he'd be when Faith left. Frowning, he pushed through the squeaky screen door. It smacked shut behind him. His dad, sitting in his wheelchair in front of the television, glanced up with a grunt, then focused on his program.

"Pops." Drake hung his hat on a coatrack carved from beech wood his parents brought back from a tenth anniversary trip. "What's Judge Judy yakking about today?" He gave his dad's shoulder a quick squeeze and sat in the armchair to his left.

His dad responded with a halfhearted shrug.

Drake gazed about the room. It was obvious the boys hadn't been here today. Their toys were gathered in a wicker basket near the fireplace. Mom's quilt, given to her as a wedding present by Great-Aunt Betty, was folded along the back of the couch, and magazines were neatly stacked on the coffee table.

The oven timer beeped, and he stood. "Guess I better see to that."

He followed the yeasty aroma into the kitchen, turned off the timer and pulled out two baking pans of golden biscuits. He moved to the window above the sink to see if he could catch a glimpse of his boys outside. A stack of mail in his parents' bill bin caught his eye.

It had grown since he'd last been over. He flipped through it. More hospital bills. Something from Hill Country Veterinarian. Two collection notices. And Drake feared that was just the beginning. It didn't help that the market had been down the past two years. Had his dad borrowed money on his land, like most ranchers did when they hit a few years of bad prices?

Drake released a heavy breath and raked a hand through his hair.

Lord, show us a way.

Tires crunched on the driveway, and he glanced up to see Elizabeth and Faith pull in one after the other. He got that strange quivering in his midsection again, like he did whenever his thoughts turned to Faith. Like he used to get when he thought of Lydia.

No other woman had stirred him since.

Until Faith. A woman he could never have.

Faith parked behind Elizabeth, then wiped her sweaty hands on her pants. She made a visual sweep of the Owenses' ranch. Cows and calves dotted the pasturelands bisected by the dirt road leading to their property. To her right stretched a sprawling, single-story house made from limestone, with a wraparound porch bordered by a weed-infested flower bed.

Two barns, one massive, the other miniature, stood to her left, and a handful of horses grazed in additional land sprinkled with yellow and blue flowers that stretched beyond.

A knock tapped on her window and she startled.

Elizabeth stood over her, grinning. "You going to just sit there all evening?"

Faith fumbled with her door and hurried out. "I'm sorry, I was just…" She inhaled the scent of sunbaked grass and dirt. "It's just so beautiful. And relaxing." At least it would be if she weren't so nervous to be spending a much too intimate evening with Drake, riding horses.

"You've never been on a ranch before?"

She shook her head and followed Elizabeth up the pebbled walk. "Is this where you live?"

"With my parents, yeah. Ever since my ex-husband left me with a bunch of debt." She stepped onto the porch. "And that, my friend, is why I decided to get a college education. Online."

"You're taking classes?"

"Was. Until Daddy's accident."

"Faith!" A high-pitched voice called out to her, and she turned to see Drake's little boys racing toward her. Mrs. Owens followed.

The oldest reached her first, his face flushed. "I've got a train set. Remote controlled." He sucked in a lungful of air and swiped at his sweaty temple. "Want to see it?"

By this time, William had caught up and was fighting for attention. "Me, too. Mine's faster." His lisp made her smile. "And yellow. That's my bestest color. Do you like yellow?"

"I do. And purple and pink and—"

"Those are girls' colors." William scrunched up his face.

Faith laughed. "Well, that's good, because I'm a girl."

The screen door screeched open, and Drake's muscular form appeared. His gaze latched on hers, and her pulse increased a notch.

"Faith." He offered that crooked smile that always made him look to be on the verge of telling a joke. "Welcome."

"Come on." Trevor tugged on her hand. "I'll show you our room—it's in the attic. That's where Daddy used to sleep."

Faith looked at Drake. "You live here, too?"

"Nah. Mom just keeps my old room for the boys, for whenever they stay over." He wasn't wearing his hat, and his caramel-toned hair was flattened, the ends curling up. A dusting of whiskers covered his jaw.

"Daddy, I want to show her my train set," Trevor said.

"After dinner. Now go wash up." He nudged his boys through the door. Facing Faith, he leaned against the side of the house, one ankle crossed over the other, and hooked his thumb over his belt buckle. "Welcome to the Owens zoo."

She laughed. "Sounds entertaining."

"Oh, they are, at that." Mrs. Owens joined them on the porch and looped her arm through Faith's. "Thanks for coming."

"I appreciate the invite. It sure beats canned apples and beef jerky."

Mrs. Owens's eyes widened. "That's what you've been eating?"

She shrugged. "The hotel doesn't have a fridge, and I can't really afford to go out to eat."

"I can imagine." Mrs. Owens eyed Drake with

a raised eyebrow. "Guess we'll have to have her over more often, won't we, son?"

Red splotched his neck, and he gave a nod. "Reckon so." He quickly disappeared into the house.

Faith followed Mrs. Owens and Elizabeth into a large kitchen with yellow appliances and wood cabinetry and floors. Cast-iron pots hung from hooks screwed into a beam that stretched above the center island.

Mrs. Owens hurried to the stove and lifted the lid of a massive soup pan. Steam billowed up, filling the air with the rich scent of roasted beef and tomatoes.

Faith hovered between the counter and the fridge, feeling in the way. "How can I help?"

Mrs. Owens cast a grin over her shoulder. "Elizabeth and I have everything under control. You go relax. Enjoy a glass of iced sweet tea."

"I, uh…" She turned to see Drake leaning against the kitchen door frame, watching her. Looking much too handsome. She swallowed. "Sure."

He straightened and moved out of the way, motioning for her to precede him. Then he met her at the table, pulled out her chair and poured her a glass of tea from a crystal pitcher.

"Thanks." This family invitation was beginning to feel much too…personal. Common sense told her to politely excuse herself, to insist upon helping the women in the kitchen. And yet here she sat, across the table from the man who held way too much sway over her pulse.

She glanced around, mainly to avoid his piercing gaze. The one that hinted at a million questions simmering just under the surface, as if he was trying to read her. "I like your home. It's warm and welcoming."

"Been in the family for six generations."

"Wow. Really? That's so cool."

He nodded. "This ranch has, at least. There's an old shotgun house on our property up a ways, built by my great-granddaddy's great-great-granddaddy."

He reached for an empty glass and the pitcher. "I get all the greats mixed up. But our family's owned this land since folks first began settling here. According to Pops, this house was built twenty-some years later. 'Course, we've added on since. Fixed things up a bit. My dad likes…" He frowned. "*Liked* to tinker with nails and a hammer. Put these floors in himself." He tapped his boot on the thick wooden planks beneath him.

"That's impressive." She opened her mouth to ask if that's where he got his love for carpentry, but his boys came barreling in before she got the chance. Soon, everyone else joined them, and the conversation took more dips and turns than Sage Creek's backcountry roads.

Faith had worried the evening would be awkward, that she'd feel out of place. But she felt oddly relaxed. And at home, like she belonged.

"Drake, will you say grace?" Mrs. Owens held her hands out, and everyone did the same until they formed a ring around the table.

Faith bowed her head, giving in to the warmth in the room, but as soon as Drake started to pray, she peeked about. Elizabeth had her eyes closed and wore a peaceful smile. Drake held his younger son's chubby fingers in his mammoth own.

Faith shifted her attention to Mr. and Mrs. Owens, who had clearly weathered and were still enduring so much, and yet were still very much in love. That was evident in the expression that filled Mrs. Owens's eyes whenever she looked at her husband, and in the way the hard lines in his face softened when he glanced her way.

A love Faith couldn't remember ever seeing in her parents.

What was the difference?

"Thank You, Lord, for holding us together, and for always giving us just what we need." Drake released her hand, leaving her to ponder his words.

For holding us together. Was that what Drake's family had that hers lacked—faith?

And yet her mom believed. So why hadn't they experienced the peace Christians talk so much about?

And how could Faith grab hold of it?

Chapter Fifteen

What was it about kids and company? Drake's boys had been acting like mini comedians all evening. Though Faith seemed amused. She'd gone from sitting there, stiff and proper, to full-on engaged.

Man, she was beautiful, with laughter sparking her eyes and adding a hint of pink to her cheeks. And when she glanced his way, her gaze snagged his and made his thoughts turn all jumbled, like a bowl of pudding that hadn't quite set.

He was looking forward to their evening horse ride way more than he should. Matter of fact, with the way that pretty little thing tugged at his heart, he'd do best to cancel. It was getting late, anyway, and the sun was starting to set.

There wasn't anything more romantic than a moonlit ride.

"Stop wooking at me!" William slammed his

pudgy fist on the table, rattling his milk glass. "Dad, Trevor keeps wooking at me."

Drake suppressed a chuckle that would only irritate his youngest more, and pushed up from the table. "Guess it's that time, huh, boys?"

They groaned, and William darted under his chair.

Drake rolled his eyes. He wasn't in the mood to go chasing after the little one. Nor was he in a hurry to leave Faith's company. But parenting came first, and the boys were clearly past their limit.

"Seems my fellas are coming unglued," he said.

Mom sprang to her feet. "I've got them. I promised them a bedtime story if they behaved."

He raised an eyebrow. "You call this behaving?"

"For a couple of squirrelly boys filled with sugar? You bet." She smiled and hurried the kids off.

Elizabeth moved toward him and, leaning forward, reached for his plate and murmured, low enough so only he could hear, "I've got Dad. You play host."

And just like that, he and Faith were left alone once again. He swallowed. Shifted. Shoved a hand in his pocket. "You still up for that ride I promised?"

Her face lit up with that heart-stopping smile

that kept weakening his resolve. But then she straightened and offered a slight nod. "Please. That is, if it's not too much trouble."

"None at all." With a hand to her back, he guided her toward the door. He grabbed his hat on the way out. A breeze stirred as they stepped onto the porch, carrying with it her familiar flowery scent. Dropping his hand, he took half a step back.

She gazed toward the afterglow of the sun as it dipped below the rolling hills in the distance. "It's starting to get dark."

"Yup."

Tiny lines etched her delicate forehead. "That's not a problem?"

"Nope." He motioned toward the well-trodden footpath cutting past the barn to the stables. "Horses have amazing night vision. Plus, they know this land almost better than I do. When I was a kid, my friends and I used to go on midnight rides at least half a dozen times each summer. We rode to the top of our land, then crossed over a patch of sagging barbed wire one of my buddies cut through."

"Trespassing, huh? Sounds like you were quite the troublemaker."

"Something like that. Till a couple of the neighbors' cows were caught wandering on an old farm road just east of here. Not sure which one of my buddies blabbed, but it wasn't long before we were all digging post holes and what-not to make up for our 'lack of sense' as my dad put it."

"That's funny."

"We pretty much stayed on our side of the fence after that."

"Pretty much?"

"Well, you know. Boys will be boys and all that." Whinnying sounded as they neared the stables. "That's my girl Baby Doll."

"That's an interesting name for a horse."

"My pops started calling her that when he was training her as a filly, on account of she always acted like such a princess. It sort of stuck." He stopped at the barrel to the right of the door to scoop up some grain. "Here. Open your hands."

Faith did, and he poured the grain in.

"Feed her this and you'll be her new best friend."

Her smile warmed him from his chest to his toes. "Thanks."

The scents of beast and fresh-laid hay reminded him of countless summers spent working alongside his dad, mucking stalls, exercising and training horses, simply walking about to give everything the once-over.

"Wow, she's so pretty." Faith stopped outside Café Latte 's stall, laughing when the quarter horse started nuzzling her shoulder. "I'd say she likes me."

He stopped and blinked away an image of his late wife riding her favorite mare at a full gallop, her hair cascading behind her.

"Any chance I can ride her?"

"That's Lydia's horse."

Faith's face sobered. "Oh. Sorry."

"*Was*. That *was* Lydia's horse. But sure. Yeah. No big deal." It wasn't that he was still mourning her. It just felt strange to think of another woman sitting on the horse his wife had trained. But then, maybe it was time. "Actually, that's a good idea. Café Latte , or Little Miss Espresso, as we've come to call her, would be perfect for you."

She chewed on her bottom lip.

"It's no problem. I promise." He stepped toward her. "To feed her, hold your hand out flat." He demonstrated.

She did, giggling when the horse's velvety lips nuzzled against her palm. This seemed to relax her some, because once the grain was gone, she started stroking the side of Little Miss's face.

"Let's get her out and saddled up."

Faith rubbed the back of her arm, her gaze shooting toward the exit and the steadily darkening sky. She was clearly spooked, a fact that triggered his inner protector.

He resisted the urge to pull her close. "I've got some glow sticks, if that'd make you feel more comfortable."

"Really?"

He nodded. "Hold up."

He dashed into the tack room and returned with the gadgets, then led the horse out of the stable. Faith followed half a step behind. "Now to get her boyfriend, Ace." He winked and tied Little Miss to the fence, then returned with a slightly aloof but obedient Bashkir Curly.

"Wow, he's beautiful." Faith ran her hand along Ace's neck.

"I bought him at a livestock auction a few months before my seventeenth birthday. He was a bit of a runt back then, one of the more reasonable horses up for sale. Still, he cost more than what I had. But my dad and I struck a deal. I'd give him all my cash, and he'd let me work off the rest."

He let out a low whistle. "Big mistake. My dad used the next six months or so to teach me what the Bible means when it says the borrower is servant to the lender."

He saddled up Little Miss while Faith continued rubbing her arm. Because she'd be riding Lydia's mare or she wasn't too keen on going out after dusk? Either way, she'd relax soon enough. And so would he. It felt strange, thinking of another woman on Lydia's mare, but it felt right, too. If anyone were to ride Little Miss, he'd want it to be Faith.

Which was absurd, considering they hadn't

known one another that long. Equally absurd was the fact that his mind kept searching for scenarios that would enable her to stay and him to date her. To allow himself to fall in love with her.

But he couldn't. Wouldn't. He refused to get emotionally involved with a woman who didn't share his beliefs. That'd be asking for trouble from every angle.

Faith waited, trying not to watch Drake's muscles flex as he saddled up both horses. He was all man, and cowboy through and through, from his faded, dirt-stained jeans to his Stetson, a fact that, at some point, had become much more alluring than annoying.

She leaned against a fence post and gazed up at the evening sky. A handful of stars had emerged, and wispy clouds shrouded a full, silvery moon. Fireflies flickered in the distance, and crickets chirped, their song merging with the gentle rustling of wind through tree leaves.

The sounds and smells reminded her of a camping trip she'd taken with one of her middle school friends.

Little Miss shifted her weight from one foot to another and started gnawing at tufts of grass on the other side of the fence. So this was Lydia's old horse. Drake hadn't seemed too keen on Faith riding her. Did that mean he was still in love with his wife?

A hollow feeling settled in her chest.

Because she felt bad for him. Not because she was falling in love with the man. That couldn't happen. She'd be heading back to Austin soon enough, back to the city and, hopefully, a thriving career.

Though a girl could get used to being out here. The fresh, clean air. Family dinners around an old oak table. Friends like Elizabeth and all the others she'd met who truly seemed to accept her as she was.

Like Drake had, even after that lanky kid had made that crack about her dad and that interview. Drake had actually taken up for her.

"Now to make you glow, baby girl." Drake activated his glow sticks, then used duct tape to attach them to the horse's breast collar.

"Those aren't very bright. Shouldn't we use flashlights or something?"

"Don't want to mess with the horses' night vision."

He plunked a short, wooden step stool on the ground beside Little Miss and motioned Faith over. "You ready?"

She gazed toward the shadowed tree line and swallowed. "As much as I'll ever be, I guess."

"This sweet girl will do you right." He touched his hand to the small of her back, as if nudging her forward. "Put this foot in the stirrup." He tapped her left leg. "Then grab the saddle horn and swing your other leg up and over."

Good thing she'd remembered to wear her tennis shoes.

He held the horse's reins while she got on, then handed them over, his fingers brushing hers. "You got this."

She offered a wobbly smile.

"How about we have a practice go-round." He grabbed the horse's bridle. "Give her a light tap with your heels."

Faith did, and the horse started to walk, while Drake led her toward the stables.

"You won't need to worry about making her turn or anything. But I could teach you if you want."

She scraped her teeth across her bottom lip. "I'd probably just confuse her."

"Another time, then." He winked and turned the horse, heading back to where they'd started.

Did that mean he planned to ask her to come riding again? Did she want him to? Unfortunately, yes.

They continued like this for maybe ten minutes, Drake guiding them around the exterior of the corral, along the outer edge of the stables, back to where Ace waited. Eventually, Faith's tense shoulders relaxed, and she loosened her death grip on the reins.

He must have noticed, because he grinned up at her. "You ready to try the trail?"

She took a deep breath and let it out slowly. "Sure."

He strolled to his horse, patted him on the rump, then mounted. He glanced back at Faith. "Remember, give her a light tap when you want her to get moving." He demonstrated and made a soft clicking noise. The horse started walking, or whatever it was they called it.

Faith followed Drake's lead past the barn and house. Golden light emanated from the dining and living room windows, and she caught a glimpse of his mom, sitting on the couch, a little one nestled under each arm. The nostalgia of the moment captivated her.

She gazed toward mounds of inky clouds hovering over the pastureland. She couldn't remember the last time she'd felt so peaceful.

Gravel crunched rhythmically beneath them as Drake guided the horses onto the dirt road leading toward the two-lane highway bordering the ranch. After about a hundred feet or so, they turned right and followed a trail dissecting a golden field. Soon this widened, and they were able to ride side by side.

"This yours?" She looked about her, taking in the serene beauty of it all, from the quiet ranch house nestled in acres of pastureland to the purple hills behind. "All this land?"

"My parents', yeah. Though I suppose it would've gone to me, had I taken up ranching."

"Why didn't you? You seem to like it."

"I was too busy acting like the prodigal. I didn't want to be under my dad's thumb, getting paid what all the other hired hands earned, any longer than I had to be. 'Course, once I started trying to pave my own way, I realized right quick how good I'd had it. But I was much too stubborn to admit it."

The trail narrowed again as they entered a patch of trees, and the ground sloped upward and grew more uneven. Branches formed a canopy above them, filtering out the dim moonlight.

A coyote howled in the distance. She gave a startled cry.

"We're all right. Night critters are more scared of us than we are of them."

She forced a nervous laugh. "I'm not sure about that."

"You okay? We can always turn back, if you want."

"No." The word blurted out before her brain had time to sensor it. At least he couldn't see the heat radiating in her cheeks. "I'm good. I'm not a complete chicken."

"Quite the opposite, from what I've seen."

Did she detect a note of admiration in his voice?

They continued on in silence for a while, the

night sounds soothing her. If only this ride could last forever.

But it wouldn't. Soon, they'd be done, as would the restoration. And she'd return to Austin, never to see him again. Maybe they'd stay in contact for a while, meet somewhere in the middle for dinner.

But those types of relationships never worked.

Besides, he had kids. That upped the complications tenfold.

She had no idea how to parent. She'd probably stink as a mom. Though Drake's boys were adorable.

They reached a small clearing, where a log shack was bathed in moonlight.

"Did someone used to live here?"

Drake swung down. "This was where our ranch began, way back when. My great-great…" He waved a hand. "Like I said earlier, I don't remember how many greats he was, but he was the guy I told you about. The one who came out here along with the rest of the pioneers."

"That's so cool."

"I don't know the particulars, but my mom's got a bunch of letters and documents somewhere. When his sons became adults, he gave them each part of the land. They built homes for their wives, had kids. Eventually, everyone but my great-granddaddy sold off their portions and moved away."

"So your property used to be bigger?"

"Oh, yeah."

"Wow. Can we go inside the cabin?"

He grinned. "Figured maybe you'd say that. It's probably a mess. It hasn't been occupied for some time, though my grandmother, something of a history buff herself, cleaned it up some. So my uncle, her middle boy, would have some place to stay while he worked on building a cabin of his own. Turned out he had zero carpentry skills and no interest in being a rancher. He sold off his chunk of land and enrolled at the University of Pennsylvania."

"So cool." The only item she had that even remotely resembled family heritage was an antique perfume bottle that, supposedly, had belonged to a distant cousin. More than likely, the trinket had been purchased at a garage sale.

"My great-granddaddy lived here for a while after he got back from fighting in World War II. He was a pack rat. Saved everything from empty bottles to old newspapers. Most of his junk's been purged. The rest is covered in dust and spiderwebs."

She grinned. "Sounds absolutely fascinating."

"I thought you might think so." He guided her horse to the post where he'd tied his, then reached out for her, palm up. She placed her hand in his, his calluses rough against her skin, his grip strong and sure as he helped her down.

His face was mere inches from hers, his gaze intense. Her breath hitched, and his eyes searched hers before dropping to her mouth.

Was he going to kiss her?

But then he straightened, as if giving himself a mental shake, and widened the distance between them. "Let's go see what treasures we can find."

Chapter Sixteen

Drake kept the log cabin's door open to allow as much moonlight inside as possible, then tapped on his phone's flashlight app.

"Great idea." Faith copied him. Then she slowly turned about, illuminating the simple log bed with dusty blanket, the cast-iron stove along the adjacent wall, the wooden cistern that was probably used to hold rainwater.

He leaned against the door frame, watching her. Clearly captivated, she ran her hand along the rough-hewn wood and fingered the trinkets, most likely placed by his grandmother, on the simple shelf.

She moved to a dust-and-cobweb-covered chest being used as an end table. "Is there anything in here?"

"Could be."

"You mind?"

He waved a hand, a grin tugging. With her

passion for history, he figured she'd love this place. What he hadn't figured was how much enjoyment he'd get from watching her.

At this moment, he was pretty sure he'd give her the world if she asked.

He straightened and swiped a hand over his face. He had to quit thinking like this.

He shouldn't have brought her here.

With a mental shake, he stepped outside and strolled to Lydia's horse. He ran his hand along her flank. Why was it the one time he thought maybe he was ready to fall in love again, it had to be with a city girl?

As if sensing his frustration, Little Miss nuzzled his shirt collar, her velvety lips tickling his neck. He laughed and scratched between her ears. Then, plucking a long piece of dead grass, he sauntered over to a partially rotting fence post and sat on the warm earth.

He waited, but in no hurry, for the sweet, fiery, beautiful woman who had somehow managed to snag his heart to emerge. Fifteen, maybe thirty minutes later, she rushed out.

He stood and dusted off the back of his pants.

"I'm so sorry." She hurried toward him. "I got a bit distracted and lost track of time."

"No problem." His gaze latched on hers, and an urge to graze his knuckles along the soft contours of her face swept over him. He swallowed and took a step back. "You ready?"

She nodded. "Your parents must be awfully worried."

"Nah. I've been night riding since I was big enough to saddle my own horse."

"Then they're probably assuming the worst."

Heat flushed his cheeks as realization of what she meant surfaced. He cleared his throat.

"I found this in that old chest." She held up what looked like an old book. "Mind if I borrow it?"

"Not at all."

"I'll give it back Monday. Tuesday at the latest."

"Keep it as long as you need."

"Oh, I'll make sure to return it before I leave. Something this old is much too fragile to travel with."

Before she left.

That day was approaching much too rapidly.

She was quiet on the ride back to the house, and he had too many somber thoughts running through his head to be of any company. Truth was, he worried what might come out if he opened his mouth. He was one breath away from asking her to stay. To leave her beloved city and become an instant mom of two very active little boys.

And if, by some crazy chance, she said yes,

they'd smack into their most insurmountable problem—she didn't love Jesus.

His kids needed a momma who did.

When they arrived at his parents' house, all but the porch and kitchen lights were off. Most likely his kids were asleep. It would be best to let them be. He'd leave a note for his mom on the table and would come see them in the morning. They'd eat breakfast together and then he'd head off to work.

He walked his horse to the fence and dismounted. After tying her to the pole, he moved to Little Miss's side where Faith sat, waiting for help down. He caught her gaze, and for a moment froze, overcome by her incredible beauty. The silver moonlight highlighted her profile and shimmered off her long, wavy hair cascading over her shoulders.

What he wouldn't give to run his fingers through her silky locks, to smell her shampoo and the soft vanilla of that lotion she always wore. To protect her from anything and everything. To provide for her, whatever she needed. Whatever would bring out her sweet, shy smile, like the one she gave him now.

"Uh…" She scraped her teeth across her bottom lip. "Can you help me down?"

"Right." Heat flooded his face. "Use the horn—" he tapped it "—for support, and swing your leg over."

She leaned forward, shifted toward him, and he laid a hand on her back for encouragement. As she swung her other leg around, he caught her by the waist and gently guided her to the ground.

Reluctant to let go, he swallowed as she pivoted to face him. Her eyes searched his.

"You're so beautiful," he told her.

Her mouth parted, and she leaned ever so slightly toward him.

Tightening his grip on her waist, he lowered his mouth to hers. She melted against him and surrendered to his kiss.

A light flicked on in his peripheral vision, and he pulled away.

She dropped her gaze and took a step back. Hugging her torso, she glanced toward the now lit living room. "I should go."

His mom's shadowed form moved past the window before the light clicked off again. Most likely she'd been in the kitchen, getting one of the boys something to drink.

"I'll walk you to your car," he said.

"That's okay, but thanks. Good night."

A blow-off if he'd ever heard one. That was for the best, all things considered, but it didn't lessen the sting.

Faith climbed into her car, resisting the urge to look back at Drake. She could still feel his hands, strong and steady, wrapped around her waist. The gentle yet firm tug of his lips on hers. And the electricity that shot through her whenever their eyes met.

She'd felt this way only once before, and it had taken her heart years, and way too much ice cream, to recover.

Unless she found a way to distance herself from Drake Owens, she was headed for a repeat.

Back at the hotel, though exhausted after the long, emotional evening that left her struggling to breathe, she tossed and turned, suddenly wide-awake. She was falling hard and fast, straight for heartbreak.

Unless…

She bolted out of bed. Unless nothing. Her life was in Austin and his was here. With his boys, his parents and all their church friends.

Could she ever be happy in Sage Creek? What about her art? The nearest gallery was over an hour away. Not unmanageable but…

This kind of thinking wasn't helping her relax. She needed a cup of chamomile tea. Since she didn't have any, she resorted to mentally naming glass colors alphabetically, until her eyelids finally grew heavy and she fell asleep.

Faith woke to the sound of birds chirping and light from the early morning sun seeping through her thin curtains. She stretched and glanced at the clock, to find it was 10:00 a.m. She hadn't slept that late since the last time Toni had cajoled her into one of her girls' nights, which resulted in Faith nursing an iced tea while her friend danced with half a dozen guys acting like fools.

She rubbed her eyes, which felt tired and gritty, thanks to all her tossing and turning the night before. Thinking of Drake's kiss, the way her heart leaped whenever he spoke her name, the ache she felt when she thought of leaving…

But she couldn't stay. Could she? Did he even want her to?

Her phone chimed, and she glanced at the screen. Toni.

"Hey." Faith sat up and leaned against the headboard. "Sorry I never called you back." She'd assumed Toni's abundance of text messages indicated boyfriend trouble, and that had been the last thing Faith wanted to talk about.

"Where you been? I must've sent you half a dozen texts last night."

"Busy."

"At 10:00 p.m. on a Friday? Spill it."

Something told her she'd need caffeine for this conversation. She shuffled to the two-cup coffeemaker and set it to brew. "What'd Mr. Romeo do this time?"

"Please. You think I'd light up your phone for

that loser?" Toni snorted. "I take it you haven't seen the news?"

She hardly ever watched television. "About what?"

"Hold up. I'll send you a link to the article."

Cup in hand, Faith returned to her bed to sift through the journal Drake had let her borrow the night before.

When he'd kissed her.

She closed her eyes, remembering the feel of his strong hands holding her steady, of his mouth on hers. The way he'd looked at her, like she was the most beautiful, most precious thing he'd ever seen, had turned her heart to mush.

"You get it yet?"

Toni's voice jolted Faith back to their conversation. "Just a minute." She clicked on her inbox. Ten messages filled her screen, the most recent from Toni. She opened it, then followed the link to an article from the *Austin Chronicle* entitled "Downtown Gallery Owner Arrested on Federal Drug Charges."

"No way." She continued reading. Police had seized over a hundred fifty boxes of documents, $110,000 in cash, along with evidence of cocaine processing. No wonder Arne, the gallery owner, was always on edge.

"They're calling it an organized crime ring."

She leaned back against the headrest. "Wow." It seemed surreal, and yet she could see it. All the high-society, private functions he held. The people streaming in and out of the gallery. "What's this mean?"

"The property's been confiscated. From what I hear, the place will likely go up for auction within the month. It pays to have handsome friends in uniform." Toni laughed.

"You're not serious." What did that mean for Faith? What about all her art displayed at the gallery—would the police confiscate that, too?

"I am. And talking with a friend with experience with this kind of thing, chances are we could snatch that place up for a crazy good price."

Faith bolted upright. "You mean bid on it? Like, to buy it?"

"Uh-huh."

Her pulse kicked up a notch as images of a renovated gallery filled with unique yet classic pieces, her work front and center among them, came to mind. "But I'm broke."

"We'll get a loan."

"My credit stinks."

"Mine's good enough for both of us."

That surprised her, considering how fly-by-the-seat-of-her-pants Toni was. But then again, she made good money. Unlike Faith, she was one of the few successful artists—those who could support themselves doing what they loved without having to travel to tackle restorations that committees might or might not have the money for.

Only to fall in love with a handsome, kind cowboy… With two kids. Who was likely still grieving, still in love with his deceased wife.

She glanced at the clock. Almost 10:30. He and his little ones would probably just be getting out of church. Mrs. Owens had asked her to come. Faith almost wished she had. Though the people at Trinity Faith were starting to grow on her, she couldn't deny that her motivation was largely to see Drake.

She was pathetic. Faith closed her eyes and rubbed her face. Why did everything have to turn so complicated? "I don't know. That'd be a lot of work."

"Doing what you love." Toni paused. "Think about it. But think fast so I've got time to get finances squared away."

"Okay." As if her brain hadn't been spinning enough. This could be big. A way to launch her career and show her dad, finally, that she wasn't a complete failure.

Or it could land her further in debt, proving the opposite.

Chapter Seventeen

Drake arrived at the church Monday morning an hour later than planned, mainly because his mom had had him running all over town to gather boxes of junk. He'd told her he'd do it after work, but she was adamant. She was convinced Faith needed every possible piece of memorabilia now, like yesterday.

If Faith found something that proved the church's murals weren't original, the committee would probably ask her to stay to restore them. That would give him more time with her—not necessarily a good thing, considering the hold she had on him.

Then there was everything tied up in the church itself. He'd grown up in this place, had gotten baptized and married here. It was where he'd looked at his wife for the last time, before her casket had been closed.

Shaking off the memory, he got out of his

truck, making a visual sweep of the property. Faith was back near the shed, hunched over that light table of hers. The one she used to cut her glass pieces on.

Hopefully she was up for some serious junk-sifting. About twenty boxes waited for her in the bed of his pickup. About half were jam-packed, the cardboard bulging due to the humidity. He could only imagine the junk crammed inside, from old family photos to random notes and pictures colored by four-year-olds. Faith was going to have quite the time sifting through it all.

Then again, she loved all things history. He smiled, thinking back to her reaction when he'd taken her to his family's long abandoned shed.

And they'd ridden together, by moonlight. When he'd helped her down off the horse, pulled her close and kissed her.

If only she lived closer. If only she was a Christian. If only she'd stick around long enough for him to introduce God to her.

Faith saw him and meandered over.

He rolled down his window. "Apparently, Lucy put word out over the prayer loop that you were looking for Sage Creek history." He pointed his thumb toward the back of his truck. "Seems my mom's not the only pack rat in town."

She stood on her toes and peered into the truck bed. "Wow."

"Too much?"

She waved a hand. "Nope. It's perfect. Thanks."

"I'll pull around to your car and load all this into your trunk for you." Except then she'd still have to cart it from her car to her hotel room. But he could help her. "Actually, I'll follow you over there after work."

He cut his engine and stepped out. "You don't have to go through it all. I'm sure the committee will be thrilled with whatever you have time for. Have you heard anything from them? About what they plan to do?"

She shook her head. "They're still trying to work out financing. If they end up repainting the entire interior, it could cost a chunk of change."

He swallowed, resisting the urge to close his eyes. Funny how attached he'd become to that tiny white building with peeling paint and scuffed up carpet.

"Drake, there you are." Miles, one of his best workers, strolled toward him. Sawdust coated his blond hair, and sweat stains spread beneath his neck and arms. "You got plans for tonight?"

"Not really. What do you need?" It wouldn't be the first or last time one of his friends asked him to help build a porch or fix a fence. He'd just tackled his parents' yesterday afternoon.

"A buddy of mine's band is playing in the Bastrop Patriotic Festival. I'm going to go check him out. Show my support and all. Wanna join? I figured we could grab a bite, heckle him some. Watch the fireworks. Maybe get to know some pretty cowgirls."

Drake's gaze shot to Faith, who was regarding him with crossed arms and a raised eyebrow. But then her tense expression evaporated behind a slight smile.

Almost as if she wanted him chasing after other ladies. To make certain he didn't go after her?

He cleared his throat. "A night of music and fireworks sounds fun. Only problem, my sister's driving my folks into Houston for an appointment this afternoon. Dad's scheduled to see the doc at four thirty, which means they probably won't get in until closer to five. Then they'll hit rush hour traffic…"

"In other words, you're out a babysitter."

"Something like that."

"What time were you needing someone?" Faith looked from Drake to Miles, then back again.

His friend shrugged. "Five? Five thirty?"

"I can do that."

"Do what?" Drake asked.

"Watch your kiddos."

"I appreciate the offer, but I'd hate to—"

"It'll be fun." She smiled. "Better than sitting in a stale hotel room."

"Well, there you go." Miles grinned and smacked Drake's arm. "This pretty little thing done stole your last excuse."

Faith. At his house. With his boys, acting maternal. An image surfaced of her sitting on the couch, a child under each arm, a book spread open between them.

He coughed and shifted. "I'm sure Faith here has plenty enough to do without trying to keep my monsters under thumb."

"Not really." She tucked a lock of hair behind her ear. "Unless you'd rather I not for some reason. I know you don't know me all that well, but I promise I won't eat your children for dinner."

"What?" She thought he didn't trust her? Great. *Way to offend a lady.* "No, that's not it at all."

She crossed her arms. "Then what's the problem?"

The woman sure seemed eager to watch his kids—so he could go out with guys and, for all she knew, snatch himself a lady. Could her lack of interest in him be any more obvious? Then again, this was a good thing. The two of them were completely wrong for each other. "No problem."

"Perfect. I'll be at your place shortly after five." She lifted her chin as if daring him to challenge her.

Man, was she something. Something he needed to stay away from, not become entangled with more.

What was she thinking, offering to babysit Drake's kids? But maybe he'd find another girl and she'd be forced to move on.

Why did that thought sting so much?

As Drake had predicted, Faith's GPS couldn't pull up his address. She was forced to follow his rather obscure directions, sketched on a piece of paper torn from a brown paper bag. She drove past the fire department for one mile, reached an abandoned gas station and turned onto a dirt road. Crossed a set of railroad tracks and continued over a narrow bridge.

Ten minutes later, she eased onto a road with more potholes than dirt. Live oaks stretched knotted branches in a canopy above her. These gave way to a clearing of dandelion-covered grass flanked by what appeared to be abandoned pastureland on one side and more trees on the other.

Drake's truck sat at the end of the gravel drive. This was the place.

The single-story cabin-like home with wood siding, green trim and a wraparound porch fitted him. A hundred yards or so past this to the right stood a small red barn just big enough to hold a couple horses.

Like Little Miss and Ace?

Did he once keep them here? It made sense, but why move them? Unless there were too many memories tied up with the animals, and it had been too painful to keep them.

Did he still love his wife? Was that something a man, if he was truly in love with a woman, could ever get over?

Obviously, otherwise he wouldn't be going out tonight. Her heart gave a sharp squeeze at the thought of him meeting someone else, but it was for the best. For both of them.

The front door squeaked open, and two little towheaded boys emerged, the smaller one leading. "Ms. Faith! Wanna pway wiff me?" He clutched a Nerf football in his chubby arms.

She laughed. Resisting an urge to gather the precious child into her arms, she gave him a sideways hug instead. He smelled of sunshine, strawberry jelly and sweaty little boy.

Drake chuckled, and she glanced up to see him leaning against his door frame, wiping his hands on a checkered dish towel. Like he'd been cooking or cleaning or something—an image she found incredibly endearing. "As you can see, they're more than a little excited to see you."

He'd shaved. Faith frowned. Dressed in a T-shirt and jeans, a turquoise-and-silver belt buckle glimmering in the afternoon sun, he looked handsome enough to catch every woman's eye.

Once again, she reminded herself that was a good thing. "And I'm excited to see the both of them." She shot Trevor a smile. "What's on the agenda, kiddos?"

The two spouted off half a dozen activities, everything from catching snakes to baking cookies. She held a hand to her chest and widened her eyes in exaggerated concern. "Baking I can handle. The creepy crawlies, I'm not so sure about."

Trevor stood half an inch taller and crossed his arms in a miniature Drake stance. "We won't bother the poisonous ones or nothing."

"Well, then." She fought to keep her expression sober. "So long as you're certain."

"Dinner first," Drake said. "Terrorizing your babysitter later."

Trevor gave an overdramatic sigh, said, "Fine," and slumped back inside. William followed, mimicking his older brother in gait and expression.

Drake shook his head. "And they say girls are the dramatic ones."

Laughing, Faith climbed the wooden steps leading to the stoop. She paused, suddenly acutely aware of Drake's masculine presence just a few feet away, and the fact that she was about to enter his personal space.

The intensity in his eyes indicated her thoughts

weren't far from his. He motioned her into the dim living room with a wide sweep of his arm. "Welcome to our humble abode, where toys are always scattered, dishes piled high and temper tantrums are only a 'no' away."

"My kind of place."

The interior held strong evidence of a woman's touch. Celery-green walls with a heather-gray accent. An old ladder turned into a shelving unit made with antiqued dresser drawers. Wicker baskets full of toys. Someone had painted the words *Live, Laugh, Love, Repeat* on the wall in elegant black letters.

"You hungry?"

Drake's deep Southern drawl startled her from her thoughts. "Huh?"

"I've got a pot of chili on the stove and a batch of cornbread in the oven."

"You cook?"

"I'm learning. Had to, if I didn't want the boys to starve. Though we do eat at my folks' quite a bit."

What would it be like to have such a strong support system? People bound to one another by the depth of love that clearly held Drake's family together. The closest thing she had to that was Toni, and to some extent, her artist friends. But as supportive as they pretended to be, most of them would turn on her for that next big commission.

"Smells wonderful." She followed him into a small country kitchen with yellow walls, dusty blue cabinets and—she blinked—Teenage Mutant Ninja Turtle curtains.

"Best chili this side of the railroad tracks, I can guarantee you that." His phone chimed. He swiped his finger across the screen and slipped it back into his pocket. "The boys will probably tell you they aren't hungry, that they hate it, or feel like they're going to throw up."

He leveled a stern gaze first at his oldest, then his youngest. "Ignore them. If they refuse to eat, put their bowls in the fridge and bring them back out when they start whining for fruit snacks later. They know the rules. No grub, no treats."

She gave a quick nod. "Any bedtime routines I should know about?"

He rubbed the back of his neck. "I hate to make you bother, though I suppose you'll get less fit-throwing if you stick to what they're used to." He set his hand towel on the counter. "We normally read a book or two, then a story from their picture Bible before they hit the hay. We always end with a prayer." He studied her. "But if you're uncomfortable with that…"

She tensed. "Uh… Sure. No problem."

She hadn't read anything biblical since…since she was eight. Strangely enough, she could still remember it. It was the story of the mother and daughter-in-law duo who had embarked on a journey of survival that ended with the younger woman falling in love with a true life hero.

She'd skipped out of her room wearing a pillow as a headdress, singing about meeting her Boaz just like the woman in the story. Her dad had sneered and accused her mom of teaching her to rely on fairy tales. And then, clutching his fancy leather briefcase in one hand and his suitcase in another, he'd left.

"Their pajamas are in the top right-hand drawer of their dresser," Drake said, pulling her from her unpleasant memories. "William sleeps in pull-ups. He puts them on himself." He guided Faith through his cluttered but cozy house, giving directions as he went. The little ones followed, showing Faith their treasures and tugging her toward their toys scattered about.

"Daddy." Trevor huffed. "Quit hogging her. She came to play with us, 'member?"

"Right." He chuckled. "I guess that's it, then." He shot Faith a wink that practically curled her toes. "You've got my number. Call if you need anything."

"Will do." She walked him to the door, his citrus cologne sweeping over her.

Before he'd so much as climbed into his truck, the boys had urged Faith outside and toward a live oak with gnarled, low-hanging branches. Laughing, she half walked and half ran to a sagging tire attached by a thickly corded rope.

As she lifted William onto the swing, Drake's engine hummed to life, and she pivoted to watch him leave. He looked back at her through his rearview mirror, waved. Then he disappeared between the trees flanking his long dirt road.

This was bad. Really bad. She was falling hard for that man, and his adorable kids. And instead of distancing herself from them, here she stood, in full-on domesticated mode.

Playing house and awakening a maternal desire she hadn't known existed so the boys' father could go traipsing about with his buddies.

Did his kiss the other night mean anything at all? Then again, she'd been the one to push him away, and run for her car with little more than a hurried goodbye. If she hadn't, would he be heading out with his friends now or would the two of them be spending the evening together?

But she wanted more than a summer romance. Could he ever love a woman like her, enough to hold tight to her? Or would he just leave when the realities of life set in and they didn't see eye to eye?

Was she willing to risk her heart to find out?

Chapter Eighteen

Faith tossed the last handful of LEGO pieces into a plastic bin and glanced at the clock. Almost 9:00 p.m. She was late getting the boys to bed. Hopefully they wouldn't be crabby or give Drake a tough time getting up in the morning.

The evening had passed so quickly. She knew she'd enjoy interacting with the boys, for an hour, maybe two, but fully expected to grow tired. And for them to grow bored with her and throw a fit. But they'd been nothing but giggles and chatter, telling her about everything from when barn owls slept to what bugs and spiders lived where.

"Let's get you both into your pj's." She returned a throw pillow to the couch, then, with one hand to the back of Trevor's head and the other to William's, guided them to their bedroom.

"Stories!" Trevor made a beeline for their little bookshelf.

"That's right." She sat cross-legged on the floor, her back against William's bed. "What one would you like to read?"

"When Monsters Go Shopping!" Trevor brought over a stack of picture books and dropped them in her lap, spouting off titles so fast he became breathless.

"This is a lot of books. How about you each choose one?"

William gave a rather adult-like nod and began rummaging through the pile. "And then Bible?"

Right.

William sprang to his feet and returned with a small, thick book with caricatures on the cover.

She smiled and released a breath. Cartoons she could handle.

They each made their story selection and sat beside her. William scooted backward until he nestled snugly under her arm.

Her heart swelled for these two. She gave them each a gentle squeeze and began reading. They knew most of the words and spoke parts out loud when she did. Once the last story had been read, she set it aside. "That was fun."

She grabbed the Bible lying on the floor and opened it. "All right. What should I read about?" She flipped to the table of contents. The story titles triggered memories of Sunday school classes from long ago. "Moses and the Burning Bush? The Crossing of the Red Sea? Jesus Calms the Storm?"

"Balaam and the Donkey Who Talks!" Trevor said, and his brother parroted him.

Interesting. She didn't remember that one. "All right. Talking animals it is."

She altered her voice as she read, going deeper for Balaam and high-pitched for the animal. The boys giggled.

But then William frowned and crossed his arms. "I want my manimals to talk to me. How come they not?"

"Uh…" How was she supposed to answer that? "I'm not sure why this happened in Balaam's case, but I don't think—"

"'Cause God wanted him to know something," Trevor said.

"Me, too?" William asked. "What He want me to know?"

This conversation was growing increasingly uncomfortable, and peppered with questions Faith had no idea how to answer. If she said the wrong thing, Drake would quite likely ban her from his kids forever.

Luckily, once again Trevor answered for her. "That He loves you and is always with you and is thinking about you and watching you all the time, even when it's really, really dark." He tried to pick up a toy dinosaur with his feet. "That's what Daddy says. Daddy says God's always talking. Through the sun, birds chirping, when people act all friendly-like and are nicer'n you thinked."

"But through a donkey?" The words popped out before her brain had a chance to stop them.

Trevor nodded. "Aunt Elizabeth says He can do what He wants whenever He wants. Otherwise He wouldn't be God."

He had her there. So many answers for such a little guy. Clearly, religion was a big part of the Owenses' lives.

Of Drake's life. That meant she and he were as incompatible as her parents had been. Except Drake seemed relaxed about the whole thing. Standing up for her, not trying to push his beliefs on her.

Beliefs like a God-turned-man who changed water into wine, walked on water and died a horrific death to somehow save her. Whether she paid Him any mind or not.

"I no hear Him." William poked out his bottom lip.

Trevor shrugged. "Maybe your heart's not listening."

Faith's chest pricked.

She gazed through the window toward the starry night sky. *You there, God?*

The house was quiet, peaceful, when Drake returned home. The television wasn't playing.

He heard nothing but the rhythmic chirping of crickets outside and the steady hum of his air-conditioning unit.

Was Faith asleep? Warmth swept through him as an image surfaced of the soft, shy smile she'd given him when he'd left. Such a beautiful woman.

He'd be leveled once she returned to Austin, which she planned to do in a couple weeks. Probably sooner.

He dropped his keys into a dish by the front door, shucked off his boots and tiptoed into the living room. Faith lay curled on the couch, the floral-and-plaid quilt his mother had made tucked up under her chin. The silver light of the moon streaming through the window caressed her face, making her look more radiant than ever.

A loose ringlet had fallen across her forehead. He stepped closer, aching to brush her hair back, to rub the silky strands through his fingers.

In their room down the hall, one of the boys sneezed, and she stirred. Her eyes fluttered open.

"Hey." He smiled down at her.

She sat up, looked around as if disoriented, then clambered to her feet. "Hi. You have a good time?"

"I did. What about you? Were the boys good?"

"They were hilariously adorable." She grabbed her purse from the coffee table and walked with him to the door.

"They're always good for a few laughs, I'll give you that." He intended his statement to sound casual, but with her standing so close to him, his voice came out husky. Almost strangled.

Way to play it cool, big guy.

He cleared his throat, then reached around her to open the door. "Thanks again."

"Anytime." She took in a short breath, her eyes filled with questions. Or, dare he hope, longing?

He shouldn't be thinking this way. He shouldn't be standing here, so close to this special woman bathed in the silver moonlight. His gaze dropped to her mouth. He shouldn't be leaning toward her.

"Faith." He cupped her jaw in his palm and urged her closer. He brushed a featherlight kiss against her lips. She responded, leaning into him. He knew he needed to step away. To go back inside and shut the door, to this, to her, to the emotions she evoked.

Instead, he pulled her closer. She made a muffled noise, then pushed against his chest. Breaking the moment and jarring him back to his senses.

"I'm sorry. I…"

Her cheeks flushed. She took a step back, as if composing herself. "Have a good night, Drake."

She hurried down his porch steps, and jumped into her car without another glance.

He released a heavy sigh and scrubbed a hand

over his face. He was in trouble. In love with a girl he couldn't have.

A girl he'd be spending most of the Fourth of July with, confined on a tiny, six-and-a-half-by-ten-foot float. With no way to distance himself from the captivating woman who had hooked him the moment he met her.

The next morning, after a night of Faith-filled dreams, Drake felt groggy and off-kilter.

"Daddy!" Trevor tugged on his pant leg. "My pancakes are smoking."

"Hmm…" Coffee mug in hand, he eyed the stove. "Oh!" He lunged toward the burner, sending hot coffee sloshing onto the floor. Luckily, not on poor little William's head. "There goes that idea." He'd promised the boys they could make flag cakes like they had at his mom's the year before. Blueberries and strawberries for decorating, a canister of whipped cream to hold everything in place.

And a mess of stickiness to clean up after.

Unfortunately, there wasn't time to make another batch. "Sorry, boys. Looks like it's cereal this morning."

He received two nearly identical groans.

"Unless you want toast. Then you can still create your Fourth of July decorations."

This produced grins and cheers, followed by

at least ten minutes with them happily occupied, allowing him to sip his coffee in peace.

Maybe not such a great thing, as his mind kept drifting to Faith and the kiss they'd shared.

His phone rang, startling him. He glanced at the screen. "Hey, Liz. Everything okay this morning?" He could hear clanking dishes in the background.

"Ask me that in about five minutes when Mom and I start coaxing Dad into the truck."

"He doesn't want to go? He loves the parade."

"He's just a bit grumpy after his appointment last night."

"What happened?"

"Let's just say the doctor gave him a stern talking to. Told him it was time to quit moping and start living."

"In other words, to accept his condition."

"That, and the real estate agent finally called back last night."

Ouch. "How bad? Will they be able to keep any of the land?" Even a couple acres would help. Let them hold on to the horses, Mom's vegetable garden.

"With no way to support it?" She sighed. "It's not looking good. We might need to take them looking for apartments."

Drake closed his eyes and pinched the bridge of his nose. *Lord, help us out here. Please.* News like that could level a man. It was all the more imperative they get their dad out of the house today. Around his buddies—guys who could make him laugh no matter what life threw at him.

"Need me to come help?" He plunked his charred pan in the sink and filled it with soap and water.

"Don't you have to be down at city hall getting ready for the parade soon?"

"Right." Matter of fact, he and the boys needed to get a move on.

The boys. The parade could take up to three hours. They'd go stir-crazy sitting on the float that long. "Uh, listen, you wouldn't mind meeting me over there, would you? To snatch up the little men?"

"That's why I'm calling."

"Thanks, sis." What would he and the boys, not to mention his parents, do without her? Though it stank for her, that no-good husband bailing on her had been the best thing that could've happened to their family. Would've been even better had he ditched her before saddling her with debt.

Elizabeth should have known, falling for a city boy. Living surrounded by concrete, high-rises and fancy restaurants did something to a person.

His mind jumped to Faith, who was different. Wasn't she?

He'd probably never have the chance to find

out, but moping about never-coulda's wouldn't help him any.

He slipped his phone into his back pocket, grabbed a rag and set to work cleaning strawberry juice and whipped cream off two very squiggly, giggly boys. Luckily, they were so excited about the parade that ushering them out the door proved easy.

When they arrived at Main Street, floats and people clogged the area. A handful of policemen were sprinkled among them. Not that anyone expected any issues, other than parking violations. But the men in blue always came out to show their support. They were as much a part of the Sage Creek Fourth of July celebrations as Wilma's Kitchen's fresh baked apple pies.

He was hankering to get a slice.

Drake parked and turned to his boys with a stern look. "No running off or acting crazy, you hear? You stay with me until Aunt Lizzy gets here. And then you need to do what she says."

William was too busy watching all the activity to respond, but Trevor huffed. He probably had his eye on the playground kitty-corner to city hall, where a handful of other kids were already climbing and running around.

Most likely Drake's boys would end up there some time or another.

He cut the engine and he and the boys got out. With his hands on a shoulder of each,

Drake glanced around for Faith. Half hoping he wouldn't see her, as unlikely as that was.

How did he get himself in this mess? He knew better than to kiss the girl. He knew having her over at his place to watch his boys would be trouble. And he certainly knew better than to fall in love with a city girl bent on returning to her artsy lifestyle. A world that for sure didn't involve someone else's young'uns.

And there was still that huge problem of her faith.

Faith, the woman without Faith. He'd find the irony humorous if he wasn't so frustrated with the whole thing.

"There you are!"

He turned to find his sister prancing toward him, her arm looped through Faith's.

When his gaze met hers, Faith's cheeks colored. But then, as she continued to study him, something else flashed in her eyes, something vulnerable, and worry lines etched her forehead.

As if maybe, just maybe, their kiss last night had awakened something in her—dare he hope, the desire to give him and his boys a chance?

But it would never work. Not with her aversion to Christianity. The Bible said not to marry nonbelievers, and with good reason. He'd seen one too many marriages derailed by religious clashes. He had no intention of adding his family to the casualties.

Chapter Nineteen

With a hint of stubble on his jaw and his Stetson shading his face, Drake looked incredibly masculine in his striped prisoner jumpsuit. Faith, on the other hand, looked absolutely ridiculous in hers. Why she'd thought pulling her hair into pigtails was a good idea was beyond her.

"Felons first." She motioned toward the space they'd kept open at the back of their float, hoping a dash of humor would ease the tension that stretched between them.

"Funny." The sober expression in his eyes contradicted his statement. He climbed on and headed straight to the front of the float, grabbed hold of the jail cell bars with both hands and focused straight ahead.

Had something happened with his dad? Except Elizabeth seemed fine. As did Drake's boys.

Just last night he'd been so warm. So…engaged. The way he'd kissed her… The way he'd held her, looked at her… She'd melted in the love and tenderness that had radiated from his eyes. Had she completely misread him?

Wouldn't be the first time. How many men had she allowed to charm her?

A whistle blew and horns honked. Music from what she assumed to be the high school marching band merged with the hum of engines. In front of them, their prison clowns motioned their driver forward, then began to skip. Their float gave a jolt, then followed maybe half a dozen others as they slowly eased down Main Street.

Men, women and children, way more than Sage Creek boasted, clogged the curbs and sidewalks on either side. She recognized a few in the crowd. A woman she'd talked briefly to that night she went to church. Another lady who'd stopped by the restoration site with lemonade and peanut butter cookies a handful of times. And—she grinned—Anna Jane, leaning against a light pole, smiling and waving like Faith was one of her best friends.

She grinned and waved back. The people here sure had surprised her, in a good way.

They weren't anything like her father said. Or like the controlling woman her mother had become. No. They were like the people Faith remembered, back when her mom first started bringing her to Sunday school.

She recalled something one of her customers

had said, a few years back. "People are people, dear. Don't go judging the God of the universe by a bunch of imperfect humans. Get to know Him, and make your choice based on that."

Get to know Him… But how?

"Maybe your heart's not listening." The memory of Trevor's words, spoken so matter-of-factly, stilled her thoughts. And stirred her heart.

The crowd laughed, and someone whooped. They must have read the sign the taller clown held, the one that begged folks for bail money. His partner, a shorter guy wearing a curly red wig and floppy shoes so big Faith worried he'd trip over them, dashed from one side of the street to the other. He held out an old, empty paint bucket.

The committee's idea seemed to be working. Nearly all the parents they passed started digging in pockets and purses for cash, which they handed off to their kids. The children ran to deposit the money in the bucket, and received a pat on the head or silly dance in return.

She laughed. "Wow. More effective than candy, huh?"

Drake glanced at her, gave a quick nod, then returned his attention to the crowd.

She suppressed a huff. Had she done something? Said something? Other than volunteering her night to watch his kids so he and his buddies could go carousing about…

Had he done something? Something he was ashamed of, while out with the guys?

She studied him, didn't flinch or look away when he caught her watching. Neither did he, but the apologetic look in his eyes made her stomach knot.

To think she'd actually been looking forward to this.

For the rest of the parade, she tried to focus on making the best of things. Mimicking Drake, she smiled and waved at the crowd, trying to distract herself from her heavy heart.

She probably should've been happy her name and website were getting out; the man driving their truck felt the need to announce it, using a blow horn, every five minutes or so. But any pride this may have warranted was annihilated by her ridiculous fake prison garb getup.

She sighed and glanced at Drake. He appeared to be doing everything he could to avoid looking at her. He barely responded to her occasional attempts at small talk. Eventually, she gave up entirely and positioned herself at the opposite side of their float. Her only consolation was seeing the steady flow of cash that parade watchers continued to toss in the clown's bucket.

Her phone chimed and she glanced at the screen. "Toni, hey. What's up?"

"I've got great news, girlfriend! I just learned yesterday—my loan's been approved! I was going to call you right away, but my phone died, and then I had this party, and, well, you know… But seriously, can you believe it? You, me, with our own gallery?"

Faith stood taller. "That doesn't mean we'll win the bid."

"Girl, you have an annoying way of always looking for the downside in everything. You really need to stop that."

She rolled her eyes. "All right, Toni. I'll get right on it."

"Sarcasm doesn't become you."

She cringed at the hurt in her friend's voice. "Sorry. It's just…"

"What? Bad day?"

"Something like that." This wasn't a conversation she wanted to be having in front of Drake.

"The restoration project not going as planned?"

"Thankfully, it is. I should be done by Wednesday, Thursday at the latest."

"Ah. Trouble in the romance department, then."

"Not everything has to do with…" Her gaze shot to Drake, and she clamped her mouth shut.

"Men? Everything worth worrying about." Her friend laughed. "Listen, I hate to splash you with this bit of sunshine and jet, but I got to go. I'm meeting a lady downtown to talk about doing a mural. Big bucks this time."

"Good luck."

The float stopped moving and she glanced up. They'd reached the end of the parade, and people crowded the street. Lucy was among them. She flashed Drake and Faith a wave and a grin. Then, weaving through the melee, she made her way to the two clowns. She was probably anxious to see how much money her idea had pulled in.

Drake adjusted his hat. "Well, guess I best go looking for my boys."

Faith nodded. "I need to grab myself some of that apple pie everyone's talking about."

Was she stupid to hope he'd offer to go with her? Instead, he told her to enjoy it, climbed off the float and started talking with Lucy and the clowns.

Faith closed her eyes against the threat of tears, took a deep breath and headed back down Main Street to Wilma's. Still dressed in her "prison garb", hair in pigtails, she received a few curious looks. But most folks simply offered a knowing smile, as if they expected to see people walking about in some sort of costume. If she hadn't been feeling so down, she may have found their playful attitudes amusing.

At Wilma's a line of waiting customers extended onto the sidewalk. Much too long on a hot, sticky July morning. Faith would come back later.

She meandered down the sidewalk, popped into a few antiques stores. Purchased a Batman lunch box. And tried, unsuccessfully, to keep her thoughts off Drake and his aloof demeanor.

Why the change? It didn't seem like him. He'd kissed her twice now, once at his parents' ranch and then at his house. It'd been obvious he had feelings for her.

And she'd pushed him away both times. In other words, she'd rejected him. She'd made it clear she wasn't interested in pursuing a relationship.

Was she? She wouldn't pursue a long-distance relationship. She'd tried that once before, and it had been a disaster. So then what? Could she live here?

She stopped outside a quaint little floral shop and glanced about. She took in the smiling children holding their parents' hands, their chubby legs taking three steps for every adult one. An older couple sat on a bench eating ice cream and talking, laughing.

Rent was probably cheaper here. And Faith could still sell her art, maybe in a Houston gallery. It wouldn't be a big deal to drive up there every month or so. She could do more online, maybe host painting parties...

What about going into business with Toni? Could she run a gallery from Sage Creek?

Could she, would she, move here for Drake?

Did she love him that much?

Yes, she did. But the bigger question was, did

he love her? Enough to build something that would last?

She didn't have time to dance around this anymore, nor did she care to. Lifting her chin, she spun on her heels and marched back toward the float area. Drake wasn't there, so she headed to the playground. She found him and Elizabeth sitting on a bench with their backs to the street.

Slowing her stride, she approached. She halted a few steps away at the mention of her name.

"Don't, Elizabeth." Drake's tone sounded weighted.

"It's time you move on. It's obvious you love her, as do the boys. They talked about her nonstop all morning." She paused. "They need a mom."

"She's not the one."

"Because she's not Lydia?"

"No. Because she's not a Christian."

Silence.

Drake scrubbed a hand over his face and turned his attention back to the playground. Back to his boys, his constant source of joy. He'd do anything for those two. Including guarding their hearts and making sure, if he ever brought a woman into their lives, she'd be the kind who'd stick around. Marriage—holding tight to a forever love—was tough enough. But starting out on opposite ends of something so important…

"Glad to know how you really feel."

He tensed at Faith's icy voice and slowly turned to face her. "Faith." What else could he say? That woman had a rather disturbing propensity to show up at the worst times.

Then again, maybe that was for the best. Hadn't he been struggling with how to close the door on their relationship?

Elizabeth stood, tiny lines stretching across her forehead. "I'm sorry…" She looked at Drake, then back to Faith. "Want to go grab an ice cream or something?"

Faith studied her, mouth flattened. She shook her head. "I appreciate the offer." Squaring her shoulders, she turned and stalked off with the same stride—hands fisted, arms swaying staunchly—as when she'd first walked onto Trinity Faith's property. After hearing she wasn't the committee's first choice.

He'd really made a mess of things. He stank when it came to women.

Chapter Twenty

Sitting in a back corner booth at Wilma's Kitchen, Faith stabbed an apple chunk and swirled it through her melting ice cream. She wasn't in the mood for pie, but neither did she want to spend the rest of the afternoon in her hotel room surrounded by boxes of other people's memories. Smiling families. Wedding pictures. Intimate relationships that seemed to constantly evade her.

Was there something wrong with her?

"She's not the one. She's not a Christian."

Tears stung her eyes as Drake's statement replayed through her mind. In other words, she wasn't good enough for him.

Hadn't she known better than to allow her heart to get tangled up in a small-town country boy? So she'd move on. Finish her job and head back to Austin.

To her empty, quiet, overpriced apartment and failing career.

She checked her phone for the umpteenth time. Jeremy Pratt from *Lone Star Gems* magazine hadn't called. Did that mean he'd nixed the feature? If he'd done any digging, interviewed the cultural committee and learned about all the questions and uncertainties surrounding the restoration, probably.

So what now? Go into business with Toni? Assuming they managed to buy the place.

If that was the only way to hold tight to her dream, yeah. She'd figure out how to run a gallery. Do whatever she needed to make it successful. To *become* successful.

"Mind if I join you?"

She startled and glanced up to see Elizabeth standing beside her table, holding a steaming mug of coffee.

Faith motioned toward the seat across from her.

Elizabeth slipped in. "It's crazy, isn't it? To see all these people in Sage Creek? Folks come from all over, some drive up to forty-five minutes, to our Fourth of July celebration. Too bad we can't get that kind of action for Settler's Day."

Faith swallowed another mouthful of pie. It landed heavily in her stomach.

Elizabeth sipped her coffee. She didn't speak for some time, though Faith could sense her watching her. Finally, she released a breath and said, "Listen, I know you're pretty upset, but we can still be friends, can't we?"

A lump lodged in Faith's throat. "That'd be nice."

"Great! So, what're you doing tonight?"

"Other than sifting through the memorabilia your mom and her friends gave me to sort out? Nothing."

"Perfect. I'll pick you up at seven." She grinned. "Tonight is Sage Creek's annual bonfire and cookout."

Hopefully Drake wouldn't be there, though Faith knew that was unlikely. Regardless, she refused to allow him being a jerk to influence her plans or get in the way of her friendships. And Elizabeth had become a friend.

"Sounds like fun."

But by that evening, her resolve and confidence began to wane, leaving a severe case of jitters in their place. She hated feeling less than. Small towns, or rather, small-town people, always had that effect on her.

A horn honked, making her jump and nearly drop her mascara wand. She checked her reflection in the mirror one last time, grabbed her purse and dashed out.

On the drive to the bonfire, Elizabeth chattered like a hyperactive teenager. She talked about where they were going, who all would be there. She shared stories of past bonfires. Faith probably would've considered most of them hilarious if she hadn't been in such a funk. But she forced a laugh or two for Elizabeth's sake.

They arrived in the middle of an expansive field at the end of a long, winding road. From the looks of it, this bonfire tradition had drawn over half the town. Growing tense, Faith surveyed the cars parked haphazardly in the grass. Drake's truck was among them.

Lovely.

"All right, girlfriend." Elizabeth grinned. "Prepare yourself for the best campfire nachos and an insane amount of s'mores."

"Sounds delicious." Once she finished digesting that giant slice of pie she'd eaten at Wilma's.

She waited while Elizabeth grabbed some folding chairs and a rolling cooler from her trunk, then offered to help carry them.

The twang of country music carried on the air along with the occasional whoop and holler coming from a group of men gathered around the back of a pickup. She didn't see Drake with them. With all the people crowding around the fire—men, women, some older, some kiddos— she couldn't tell where he was.

She shouldn't be looking for him at all. Except that she wanted to avoid him.

Elizabeth stopped about two hundred feet

from the bonfire. On either side of it, two smaller fires burned and were being used for cooking.

She planted her hands on her hips. "This look like a good place?"

Faith deposited the chairs she'd been carrying. "Works for me." She was glad Elizabeth didn't want to be in the throng of people.

A faint crescent moon emerged with the sun's descent, and the temperature dropped from oppressively sticky to pleasant and breezy. The scents of char-grilled meat and campfire smoke wafted toward her.

Elizabeth leaned back in her chair and stretched her arms to the sky, then dropped them. "You ever been to a pig roast?"

"Once, when I was nine. It freaked me out a little, seeing that adorable little creature impaled, snout, eyes, and all."

"You poor thing. You must've been traumatized."

Faith laughed. "Nothing intense therapy can't fix."

"You want a Coke?"

"Sure."

Elizabeth opened the cooler sitting beside her and pulled out two cans. She handed one to Faith, then settled back in her chair. Face angled toward the sky, she closed her eyes. "This is exactly what I needed."

Faith played with the tab of her Coke and

watched a couple who appeared to be in their midforties play Frisbee. The woman, a petite lady with short blond hair, couldn't toss the thing straight or far, while the man appeared to gain great satisfaction from hurling it over his wife-girlfriend-whatever's head.

"Aren't they adorable?"

Faith looked at Elizabeth. "Huh?"

"That's Eric and Amanda. They were high school sweethearts. They've been married for going on twenty years, still living and loving like newlyweds."

So, apparently, love did last for some. What she wouldn't give to know their secret.

"About what you overheard back at the park…" Elizabeth set her Coke in her chair's cupholder.

"It's no big deal." And certainly not anything Faith cared to talk about. If she did, she might cry, and she wasn't about to turn into a snotty-nosed, sniffling, raccoon-eyed mess in front of these people. How did she manage to fall so hard so fast?

She'd known better.

"It *is* a big deal." Elizabeth leaned forward, her brow furrowed, her eyes searching Faith's. "You were hurt, and I don't blame you."

"He's not interested." Or rather, thought her beneath him. "It happens."

"Quite the opposite, actually. I'm pretty sure he's in love with you."

Faith snorted and looked away. "Right. Like he doesn't have his own garbage cluttering his kitchen."

"Oh, he's got plenty of garbage. The difference is he's got Someone to help him take it out."

"Listen, you want to talk about this, fine. But can we drop the riddles?" She took in a deep breath and spread her hands flat on her thighs. "I'm sorry. I don't mean to be so snarky, it's just…"

"You're speaking from a broken heart."

Faith gave a hiccuped sob and pressed a fist to her mouth. She blinked until the threat of tears subsided.

Elizabeth reached for her hand. "I know it's hard to understand, but Drake's faith is important to him. It's the power source that keeps a couple together when everything else pulls them apart. And…" She paused. "It was the foundation that held him together as he watched his wife lose her battle to cancer. Without Jesus, he would've fallen apart."

"If that's true, then my parents should be married now. My mom's a Christian."

"But your dad's not, right?"

She snorted. "Hardly."

"That cause a lot of tension between them?"

"To put it mildly."

Elizabeth gave a slight shrug. "I suspect that's why the Bible warns people not to marry those who don't share their faith. It can create a whole truckload of problems."

Faith thought about Elizabeth's words the rest of the night, about Christians marrying non-Christians and all the fighting she'd witnessed between her parents. Of Drake and what he must have gone through, losing his wife. Of what his parents were going through right now.

She'd heard people talk about God's love getting them through tough things, but had no idea what they meant. Honestly, she'd assumed those were simply words, like all the other Christian slogans tossed about on Facebook. But what if there was something more?

She gazed up at the sky, taking in the vibrant red, orange and purple streaked across the horizon. She felt a tug on her heart, and a desire to know more. To somehow grab on to the peace, joy and…and whatever it was Elizabeth and her family seemed to have.

That night, unable to sleep and unwilling to think about Drake, his family or their faith, she dug through boxes one by one. Most were filled with junk. Old magazines. Ticket stubs to movies, plays and sporting events that probably held great value to the owners, but didn't help Faith in her quest to uncover the church's original painting job.

She removed items piece by piece, laying them carefully in front of the box from which they came. Her gaze kept shifting to one labeled Owens, and her heart gave a painful squeeze. Drake's history, his lineage, preserved for who knew how many generations.

She resisted the urge to sift through its contents, but the box kept drawing her eye. Finally, somewhere between 2:00 a.m. and sunrise, she sat surrounded by old family photo albums, newspaper clippings of Drake's football days and other random items that had to be at least fifty years old.

She picked up the leather-bound book she'd taken from the shack on the Owenses' property. It appeared to be a journal of some kind, with sharp, cursive writing, chunks of which were smudged.

She began to read the entries.

"I felt certain You called me here, Lord. That You called all of us to this project. I invested all my time and savings into building that church. We all did. And now that it's almost done, to walk away, as if I had no part of it. And for what? A moment of indiscretion, one that not only deeply hurt my wife and our children, but nearly destroyed our faith community. How could I, an elder and one of the founding men in this project, have been so stupid?

"I suppose I could attempt to talk my way

out of this, maybe even convince everyone to let me remain on the project. But that would only cause my family more pain, nor do I want my sin overshadowing all You want to do with that building, Lord. I fully believe the story of this church, erected by my countrymen, will be told for generations. When it is, I want to make certain the sacrifice of all involved, and not my behavior, is what this endeavor is remembered for.

"I'll bring my sketches to Pastor Ellison tomorrow and respectfully step down.

"I thank You for Your grace. I know I haven't acted like I should. Forgive me, and help me do better. Help me act like a child of Yours should."

She thought again of Elizabeth's words, spoken hours before. Of her mom, and all the Sunday mornings she'd dragged Faith to church. Of her father's snide and biting comments once they returned.

He'd been such an angry, short-tempered man. If she were honest, it wasn't Mom's religion that broke her parents apart but her father's anger toward it. How different would things have played out if he'd accepted one of her many invitations to join her at church? If he'd listened when she'd talked about her love for Jesus and all He'd done? If he'd recognized his weaknesses and asked for forgiveness, tried to change, like the man in this journal?

All these years, she'd been holding God accountable for her father's decision, because that had been easier. Back when she still wanted to believe her father was good and kind and loving. Back when she'd begged God night after night to bring her parents back together and it felt like her prayers had landed on deaf ears.

What if He'd been speaking to her, reaching out to her, all along, but her heart simply hadn't been listening?

Show me who You are. Teach me how to know You. Like Elizabeth and Mrs. Owens do. Like Drake does.

She returned her attention to the yellowed pages before her. Verses and expositions followed, interspersed through the man's writings, showing tentative, then stronger, steps to faith.

She glanced at the date written above an entry: 1859. Around the time Czech and German immigrants came to Texas and began creating the beautiful painted churches. Had they intended Faith Trinity to be one of them?

She flipped through the pages, reading snippets and dates—about Sage Creek, the church, the ranch. Nearly halfway through, she came upon several illustrations—preliminary sketches. For Trinity Faith?

Who was this guy, anyway?

She turned back to the inside front cover. Clarence Owens.

She pulled up the internet on her phone and typed his name into the browser. She spent the next thirty minutes scanning various articles. Nothing. But then again, why would there be? According to his journal, he'd abandoned the project and maybe even got himself kicked out of church.

And yet she was holding in her hands a piece of previously undiscovered history, complete with dates, times and locations.

This could be precisely what the cultural committee needed to get the church listed on the historical registry. It might even gain enough publicity to salvage her dying career.

Could it also provide the way for the Owenses to save their ranch?

Chapter Twenty-One

Drake watched his parents closely, doing his best to keep his emotions in check. They sat side by side, his dad in his wheelchair, his mom in the adjacent chair. She kept her hand on his, her eyes focused on Mr. Brewer, their accountant and longtime family friend.

Mr. Brewer shifted and cleared his throat. "Normally in these situations, I'd suggest filing for Chapter 12, but you'd need to be able to pay your creditors back within three to five years. Unless the courts approve a longer time frame, but even then…"

His folks would need to pay the money back sometime, and with Dad tied to his chair…

Dad slammed his fist on the table. Mom jumped, and tears filled her eyes. Mr. Brewer winced, looking about ready to hightail it out of there.

"All right." Drake tried to catch his dad's gaze, needing to calm the man down so he could do what he needed to do, for Mom's sake. "Let's everyone take a breather. There's a lot of information to process—"

"We've been processing long enough." Mom's tone was low but firm, and she leveled a look at her husband. "I know this is hard. It's not fair. I know how hard you've worked for this ranch. I know how much this land, this home, means to you, to all of us." Her voice cracked. "But sometimes a person's got to do what a person's got to do."

Drake hated to see his mom in such pain, to see his dad looking so…helpless. Dejected. His hero, the man he had, growing up, seen as invincible, now unable to provide for his family.

His mom scooted her chair to face her husband and took his hands in hers. "It's time. We've had a good run, and made some wonderful memories. We've built a strong marriage and family. Let's hold tight to the things that matter most."

Dad covered his face with his hands, his body shaking with silent sobs.

If only there was something Drake could do. Some way to help.

He could give up his contracting business. Take over the ranch, like Dad always wanted.

He winced. He'd built his business from scratch. But it was the only solution that made sense.

Taking a deep breath, he stood. He walked to

the breakfast counter and leaned against it, arms crossed. "There's one other—"

The doorbell rang. "I've got that." He needed a moment to strengthen his resolve.

With heavy steps, he crossed through the living room. He answered the door, to find Faith standing on his parents' porch dressed in a faded T-shirt and jean shorts. Her hair framed her face in long, loose curls. Her chestnut highlights glimmered in the sun, and a slight pink tinged her cheeks.

Standing here now, looking so beautiful, she represented yet another loss.

"Hey." He leaned against the door frame.

"Your parents okay? You weren't at work today."

Was that why she'd stopped by? That was sweet, and evidence of her tender heart. The kind of woman he'd love to marry, to bring into his boys' lives. If only she shared his faith.

"Finished early."

"Drake, who is..." His mom emerged from the kitchen. "Faith, how good to see you." She approached her with arms wide and a somewhat tense smile. Being the Southern host that she was, she wouldn't turn Faith away. At least, not without offering her sweet tea and a home-baked cookie.

"Come in, dear." His mother motioned Faith inside.

They'd pretty much concluded their meeting with the accountant anyway.

Drake knew what he needed to do.

At the cost of his business. There was no way he could manage both. Nor was there any guarantee he could keep his parents' place afloat. They'd accumulated a lot of debt.

"Like those famous painted churches throughout Texas?" The lift in his mother's voice pulled his focus to her and Faith's conversation.

Faith sat, her eyes bright. "I think that was the original intent, yes. But the project got disrupted by some sort of internal tiff."

His mother perched on the edge of the armchair across the coffee table from her. "So you're saying..." Her gaze slid to Drake's, the hope in her expression evident, before shifting back to Faith. "...we have an important artist in our family tree, one who lived right here on the ranch."

"Exactly." She went on to explain information she'd uncovered and what that meant.

Mom brought a hand to her mouth. "Our place is historical?"

Elizabeth and Mr. Brewer entered the room.

Drake stepped closer. "So what's that mean? Will we be able to list it at a higher price, get more money when we sell it?"

Faith's eyes widened. "Don't do that."

Mom frowned and stared at her hands.

"They might not have a choice," Elizabeth said.

Faith turned to his mom. "What if you renovated this house into a bed-and-breakfast? And really played up the historical part?"

Elizabeth squealed. "We could have horseback riding, and dress colonial. Maybe sell some acreage, but not all, and the cattle."

Drake scratched his jaw. This could work. "My buddy Neil's looking for property for an outdoor adventure type thing. Bet he'd be interested." If anyone were to buy their land, he'd want it to be Neil. He was about as close to family as someone could get without being blood related. "He wouldn't try to lowball us, either. Plus, you wouldn't have to sell it all. You could keep the stables and arena, ten acres for grazing."

Mom brought her twined fingers to her mouth, her eyes brimming with hope.

"This could be so awesome," Elizabeth said. "We could spiff the place up. Make it match the historical period." She grabbed Faith's hand. "You could help."

Mom' s eyes grew misty. "Faith, I could just squeeze the stuffing out of you, girl."

So could Drake. Matter of fact, it was taking all his self-control not to draw closer to her and kiss that beautiful, bright-eyed face of hers.

If only...

He shifted to face Mr. Brewer. "What do you think? Does this sound viable?" This could be exactly what his folks needed to keep their place *and* pay off their debts.

Mr. Brewster tugged on his earlobe. "I think you've got some phone calls to make—to your buddy, the cultural committee, and maybe the historical society. But yeah." He chuckled, the heavy lines that had etched his face only moments ago now gone. "This could really take off."

Elizabeth squealed again and snagged Faith in a hug. Their mom joined in. Drake lunged forward, his heart full, drawn into the moment. But then common sense caught up and he stopped, his gaze locked on Faith's.

A flash of sadness filled her eyes. With what appeared to be a fortifying breath, she looked away.

He hated knowing he was the cause of her pain.

Faith checked the time on her phone. "We should get going." She avoided glancing Drake's way, knowing if he made eye contact, she'd come undone. And she had no intention of showing up to the committee meeting puffy-eyed and snotty-nosed.

"Right," Drake said. "I'll call—"

Mr. Owens wheeled in. "What're y'all yapping about in here?"

"Faith found a way to save our home, Daddy." Elizabeth grinned.

"Don't go counting your calves before they're birthed, now." Drake snatched his hat off the rack. "There's still a lot of details to work out. I need to see what Neil might be willing to pay for the land—"

"Wait a minute." Mr. Owens's scowl deepened as he shifted his focus to his daughter. "I thought you said we were keeping the place."

Mrs. Owens placed a hand on his shoulder. "We are, dear. At least part of it. Enough."

"I'll leave you two to talk things out." Drake winked at his mom and gazed out the window. "Can y'all keep an eye on my rascals?"

They were playing with the water hose and covered in mud and grass.

With the ninety-plus temperatures they'd been having, Faith almost envied them.

"'Course." Elizabeth gave a thumbs-up, then gave Faith another hug. "Thanks, girl. I can't tell you what this means. For my parents, for me. For all of us."

"I got lucky, I guess."

"No luck about it. You've helped provide the answer to countless nights of prayer."

Faith dropped her gaze and tucked her hair behind her ear.

Could Elizabeth be right? Could God have used Faith, her coming here, her love of history, the patch of peeling paint on the church wall— all of it—to save the Owens Ranch?

And what if she talked to Him? Like Elizabeth and Drake did. Would He listen? Maybe even help her?

She met Elizabeth's gaze. "Do you think your pastor would be willing to meet with me? I've got questions. About… Jesus."

"For sure! I'll call him now." She had the pastor on the phone before Faith made it to the porch.

Elizabeth followed her to her car. "Tonight work? At Wilma's."

"Perfect." A sense of expectation filled Faith's heart as she slid into the driver's seat. It still hurt, the way things had turned out between her and Drake. But she had a feeling, almost like a knowing, that she was about to get something even better.

Something no one—not Drake, not her dad, not a failed project or career—could take away.

As usual, the cultural committee meeting was being held at the high school. Unless the team decided to repaint the church's interior, this would be the last one. And by Friday, if not sooner, Faith would be packed up and headed back to Austin.

Never to see Drake or his boys again.

How had she grown so attached to those three in such a short period of time?

She blinked back tears as she pulled into the high school parking lot. *Lord, I have to believe You're in this.*

Taking in a deep breath, she cut the engine and stepped out into the hot, late afternoon sun. The scents of chicken and charcoal drifted toward her, the squeal of giggling children and the yapping of a dog merging in the distance.

The sounds and smells of a happy, nostalgic summer. It made sense why so many people loved small towns. She'd come to feel the same. She could even envision herself living here, if not for Drake. She wasn't sure her heart could handle seeing him every day, so close yet out of reach.

Cold air swept over her, sending goose bumps up her arms, as she stepped inside and made her way toward the cafeteria. As usual, Lucy and her gang were already seated around one of the long, rectangular tables. The mayor and Drake were there, as well. She could feel their eyes track her as she made her way across the room.

She settled into a vacant spot kitty-corner from Lucy. "Hello."

Lucy smiled and folded her hands in front of her. "I received your email regarding what you found."

"Do you think it'll help?" Faith said.

"It might. It certainly makes for a great story— a potential start to one of Texas's famous painted churches, abandoned, then later resumed and… well, changed. Though the truth is, we don't have money to pay for a complete redo."

Then Lucy brightened. "But from what Drake's

been telling us, Sage Creek might still have a claim to fame."

"Yes." The mayor grinned. "Tell us more, Faith. About what you discovered. What it means."

She did, beginning with the journal she'd read, all one hundred plus pages of it.

"Glory be." A short man with a shiny bald head—Faith could never remember his name—chuckled. "That's quite a story! Of one man's moral failure—"

"But ultimately, of the overriding power of grace." Lucy lifted her chin. "That church was built, if not how those immigrants wanted, then how it was meant to be. And it's remained standing through tornadoes, economic crises, religious spats and the recent fire."

And so it had.

"So, what do you think?" Drake glanced from face to face, his eyes hopeful.

"I'll make some calls." Lucy flipped her notebook closed. "See what y'all need to do to get the ranch listed in the historical registry and if there are any preservation laws to consider. You might even qualify for a 20 percent tax credit, when y'all start rehabilitating the place. I assume you'll be doing some of that."

"Most likely." Drake looked ready to jump up and whoop and holler.

"Regardless, I don't see why y'all can't carry out your business plans," Lucy said. "Whether the place gets listed officially or not, we know the history. You've got the letters and such to prove it. Build a website, mount your 'proofs' so to speak, where folks can see them, and enjoy the blessings of God's provisions."

Drake grinned like a kid on his birthday. "Sounds like a plan. Now, if you'll excuse me, I need to call my buddy to see if he might be interested in buying a parcel of my folks' land."

Faith watched him go, thankful for how things had turned out, for the most part. She'd made some great friends, and had even started communicating with God again.

Though she'd be leaving here with a broken heart, she sensed she'd also be taking the first steps to healing and wholeness.

Chapter Twenty-Two

Drake parked in front of Wilma's and called Neil. "I've got some good news for you, bro. Can you meet over coffee and apple pie?" He tipped his hat at one of his mom's friends walking down the sidewalk.

"I'm always up for dessert. Wilma's?"

"Yep."

"I can be there in ten."

Inside the diner, the enticing scents of buttery crust, cinnamon and roasted garlic caused Drake's stomach to rumble, reminding him that he'd skipped lunch. On account of the family meeting he and his mom had planned. To think he'd worked himself up to being nearly sick, when God had a solution all along.

Then again, it wasn't a done deal yet. Though Neil would be a fool not to jump on his offer.

"Hey, cowboy." Sally Jo sauntered over with

enough hip sway to do the hula. "You eating by yourself today?"

"Nope." He knew what she was implying. "I'm waiting on someone."

"I see." Her smile evaporated. "Can I get you something to drink while you wait?"

"Coffee will be fine."

Neil arrived before Drake finished half his cup. "Tell me what's so awesome you interrupted my workout."

"I would've waited for you to clean up." Drake leaned back and wrinkled his nose, then laughed. "You still looking for land for that adventure area/obstacle course you want to build?"

"Yeah. I've checked out some places, but they're either overpriced or too far out. I need land close enough to make it a church camp and family reunion site. I doubt I'll get enough business with extreme sports enthusiasts alone to keep the place up and running."

Drake couldn't suppress his grin.

"Uh-oh." One side of Neil's mouth quirked up. "I know that look. Let's have it. Tell me about your clever plan to help me launch my dream."

Drake shared his ideas regarding his parents' property and suggested a sale price—one that would enable his parents to cover their medical debts and get the bank off their backs. While making sure they retained a steady flow of income—and a chunk of their property.

"Almost like a partnership then." Neil rubbed the back of his neck.

"Sort of. Except you'd each manage your part autonomously. My parents would run the bed-and-breakfast and stables. They could probably cater some meals or whatnot, depending on group size." Mom's kitchen had been big enough to feed all the ranch hands, back when Dad's business was thriving, and a whole host of church lady functions.

"I love the trail riding idea, and having someone else to manage the horses would be nice. It'd free my time to lead adventure groups, do youth events, whatever. And the price is fair." He drummed his fingers on the table. "Think you'd help me out with the building?"

"I had a feeling you'd try to rope me in somehow."

"Hey, that's your thing."

"It is." He'd loved carpentry since he was a boy. Ever since his dad taught him to wield a hammer. "And I will."

Neil slapped the table. "Let's do this thing."

Drake laughed, aware that all eyes in the diner had turned on them.

"With that settled…" Neil grabbed the water glass Sally had set on the table. "Tell me about that cute little girlfriend of yours. You talk her into relocating to our beautiful county yet?"

Drake's heart pinched. "She's not my girlfriend, and as far as I know, she's heading back to Austin tomorrow."

The bell above the diner door chimed, and he glanced up to see Faith enter. She made a visual scan of the room, met his gaze, sucked in a breath, then looked away.

As if it pained her to see him.

He sighed and, lifting his coffee mug, focused on his prattling friend, who'd launched into a full-on exposition of his building plans. Drake resisted the urge to go to Faith, to beg her to be with him forever.

If she were to say yes, pain would follow—for him, for her, for his boys—when everything fell apart. That would hurt a lot more than anything he was experiencing now.

Of course Drake had to be here. Looking so handsome, the way his eyes softened when they met hers, and his thick brows pinched, like they always did when he was working through a problem.

She wanted to be mad at him. Then his rejection wouldn't sting so much. But she couldn't blame him. She of all people understood his concerns, having watched her parents' marriage fall apart over different belief systems.

What was it the pastor had said at the midweek prayer meeting? *"Whether you accept or reject God's free gift of salvation is completely up to you. But this decision mustn't be taken lightly. Your eternity rests on it."*

She'd given that a lot of thought, and she felt ready to make a decision.

The front door chimed open, and Pastor Roger whooshed in like a blast of color, all smiles and energy. He gave Drake and his friend an enthused wave, then continued to Faith, greeting nearly everyone en route.

"Faith, good to see you." He slid into the booth across from her. "Hope I didn't keep you waiting."

"The waitress hasn't even been by yet." She didn't mention it seemed like Sally Jo had been intentionally avoiding her. Apparently, she still considered Faith a threat. She'd find out soon enough that Drake had dropped her like a charred slice of pie.

"Good." He grabbed one of the menus. "Don't know why I bother looking at this. I always get the same thing."

Faith smiled and started to ask for food recommendations when Sally approached.

"Pastor, good to see you." Her smile looked tight. "What can I get you?"

Faith's budding excitement, akin to what she felt when embarking on a new art project, had dulled her appetite, but she ordered a brownie sundae anyway. The pastor asked for a cheeseburger with fries.

He took a sip of water. "Elizabeth said you had some questions for me?"

Faith ran her thumbnail down the fold of her napkin. "More than I know how to voice."

"Take your time."

"I don't know if it's a question so much as…" She traced the edge of her napkin. "I… I want the peace and joy Drake and his family have. I mean, I know they get upset, and they have to be stressed out, with everything going on with Mr. Owens and their ranch. But even in that, they act different, you know? Like they're at peace. And I want that."

"The calm you see comes from their relationship with Christ."

"Yeah. That. I want that."

"That's great to hear." And then, using Scripture, he filled in all the blanks Faith had held for so long, until she finally understood.

"You ready to pray with me? To take a step of faith into faith, Faith?" Mirth crinkled the skin around his eyes.

She nodded, feeling a little jittery. Like she'd swallowed a pound of sugar or something.

Or maybe was about to make the most important decision in her life. One she knew, without a doubt, she'd never regret.

"All right, then, let's talk to your new best friend now."

As the pastor prayed, Faith felt as if a dark,

heavy weight she'd been carrying lifted. And in its place came peace and…dare she say it? Joy.

"Now what you need is a Bible." The pastor tucked a twenty-dollar bill beneath his plate and stood. He raised a finger, then approached Drake's table. "Would you mind taking our friend Faith to the Literary Sweet Spot to get her a Bible?"

Faith's cheeks heated, and her heart gave a jolt at the spark in Drake's eyes. As if the pastor had just offered him a long-awaited gift.

Pastor Roger handed over a credit card. "The church will pay for it. Make sure they engrave today's date, the day she crossed over from death to life, on the bottom right-hand corner."

Drake's gaze zinged to Faith, and he gave that slow, easy smile that always weakened her knees. "I'd be honored."

His expression, so tender and loving, stole her breath.

Almost making her forget about the conversation she'd overheard, the one where he'd said he couldn't be with her.

Because she wasn't a Christian.

Except now she was.

Did that mean…?

No. She couldn't think that way. She had most of her stuff packed, her job at the church was completed except for reinserting a couple windows, which she'd do first thing in the morning.

By Friday, she'd be gone. Ready to move on, doing her best to forget all about Drake and his adorable little boys.

Chapter Twenty-Three

Drake stumbled to his feet, unable to voice the jumble of words swarming his brain. Faith? A Bible?

Once again, God had come through. Twice in one day, first with his parents' ranch and now this.

His gaze swung between Faith and Pastor Roger, his heart so full it felt as if his chest were expanding. He smiled. "There's nothing I'd rather do." Well, that wasn't quite true. What he wanted most was to grab the beautiful woman in his arms and kiss her silly.

"Are you sure?" She picked at her pinkie nail. "Because—"

He grabbed her hand. "No, really. It's an honor." And an answer to so many prayers. Some he hadn't even realized he'd had, until he laid eyes on this precious creature.

Color sprang to her cheeks, and she dropped

her gaze for a moment before lifting her gray eyes to his. "Thanks."

"My pleasure."

She glanced at her hand, still held securely in his, and heat climbed his neck.

He let go and cleared his throat. He turned to Neil and dropped some cash on the table. "Guess you'll call me later?"

"Yep." Neil stood. "Tell your folks to expect an offer by tonight."

He grinned, feeling like a kid who'd just won a trip to Florida. Of course, his dad still had to buy in to the idea, but Drake wasn't concerned. His father was a smart man. He'd realize what a blessing this was.

Lord, please make that be true. He slid his wallet into his back pocket and touched Faith's elbow. "You ready?"

She nodded, and he led the way out of the diner, holding the door for her. A handful of cars were parked along the street as townspeople trailed in and out of storefronts. A couple teens with baggy jeans and bangs flapping in their faces whizzed by on skateboards.

A car hummed by, and they paused on the curb. When it passed, Drake nudged Faith forward with his hand on the small of her back. He longed to twine his fingers through hers, but feared that'd be too forward.

They needed to have a talk. Didn't they? Could they? Or was it too late for that?

Surely God wouldn't stir Drake's heart for this woman, then clear away the barrier that kept them apart, only to snatch her away.

Mrs. Mitchell, the owner, greeted them as they entered the Literary Sweet Spot.

Drake tipped his hat to her, then led Faith toward the far back corner. "Bibles are this way." He picked up one with a purple cover embellished with swirls and flowers.

She looked about, eyes wide. "I want something easy. Do they come like that?"

"How about a devotional? Or maybe one of these question-and-answer books." Why on earth did Pastor Roger think Drake should be the one to help Faith pick this out?

Maybe this wasn't just about the Bible.

He returned the Bible to the shelf, fiddled with his hat. "Listen, about what I said at the park the other day—"

She raised a hand. "I get it."

He studied her. "You do?"

She nodded. "Your faith's important to you. As a person and a father."

"I don't want to sound rude or anything, but... what happened?"

She fingered the spine of a blue prayer journal. "I guess my heart finally started listening."

Lydia used to say something similar. Said that

was her biggest prayer for him and their boys, for their family—that their hearts would always listen for the quiet voice of God. Because, she said, so long as they did that, everything else would have a way of working itself out.

Faith's phone rang, and she glanced at the screen. "It's your sister." She answered. "Hey. Long time no see. Really? That's awesome! I'd love to come." She ended the call and slipped her phone into her purse.

Drake's cell trilled less than a minute later. "Elizabeth?" He chuckled. "You checking up on us or something?"

"More like cashing in on all my IOUs."

"I'm not sure I like the sound of that."

"I'm pulling about ten pounds of ribs out of Dad's deep freezer. Would you mind grilling them up tomorrow? Mom and her friends are making a slew of baked goods—"

"What's the celebration?"

"The day my big brother saved the ranch."

"Neil called?"

"He did. Mom and Dad are meeting him at the bank tonight to make it official."

Drake gave a holler, startling Faith and causing numerous heads to turn their way.

He ended the call. "You find something?"

She nodded and lifted a Bible with a floral cover. "I should buy this and then get going. I need to be packed and checked out of the hotel by two tomorrow."

His heart ached. She was leaving. Tomorrow. Probably as soon as the party was over.

A celebration and goodbye rolled into one.

Though he'd dated his fair share of women, he'd loved only two. He lost the first to cancer, and the second he was about to lose to a big city with fancy restaurants and high-rises.

The next afternoon, Faith slowed as she neared Drake's parents' house. She stared at all the cars and people. This was more than a little barbecue. It looked like nearly the entire town had come out, and, based on all the pretty bags stuffed with tissue and all the wrapped boxes stacked on the picnic table, most of them brought gifts.

Tears sprang to her eyes. It felt good to be here, with the Owenses and the other folks from Trinity Faith. She couldn't remember when she had last felt so welcomed and loved, and these people truly did love her. At least Elizabeth and Mrs. Owens did.

What about the latter's son?

She scanned the crowd for Drake. Found him standing over a large black grill, dressed as usual in his Stetson, a snug T-shirt and blue jeans.

With a deep breath, she checked her hair in the rearview mirror, then stepped out.

"Yay!" Elizabeth hurried toward her. "If it

isn't the town hero." She looped her arm through Faith's. "I hope you're hungry, because Mom and her friends went all out."

She motioned toward a second table, not terribly far from the first, covered in all sorts of bowls and platters, and started walking that way.

Faith smiled and matched her step. "I could eat." She stopped. "But you all are really making me out to be something I'm not. I simply stumbled upon a journal."

"With information that saved the ranch and, God willing, will put Trinity Faith on the map. Or at least make it the subject of some really cool newspaper articles. Maybe even a television documentary."

Which meant Faith might get a feature in *Lone Star Gems,* after all. Wouldn't that be wild?

Soon she was enveloped in more hugs and showered with more thank-yous than she knew what to do with. Her brain couldn't make sense of it all, or even who was talking when. Luckily, everyone settled down and started eating soon enough. All except for Drake's boys who, after giving her a quick hug, darted off to chase frogs and snakes.

"They'll be back," Drake said. "Soon as Mom cuts into the cake."

"Faith…" Mrs. Owens took her hand in both of hers. "I don't know how to express my gratitude. Just when I'd mourned and surrendered this place." She motioned toward her home. "God handed it back to me. Thanks to you."

"I, uh, I'm glad everything worked out."

"Still can't believe it." Drake's friend Neil shook his head. "To think we close in two weeks, and I'll finally have a chunk of land to start building on." He wiped his mouth with a napkin and shifted to face Drake's dad, who for once didn't look so surly. "I really appreciate this, sir."

Mr. Owens gave a quick nod, his eyes misty. "My son not included, it couldn't have gone to a better man."

Everyone started clapping. Soon they were swapping stories of everything the church, ranch or town had weathered since the first handful of settlers put down roots, or how residents had found their own plot of earth.

"Now if we could just talk Faith here into staying a little longer to help us refurbish this place…" Mrs. Owens winked at her.

Faith forced a laugh. "If you'll excuse me." She went to grab a bottled water from the cooler near the house.

Drake ambled over. "You've sure done a lot of good here."

"Guess my curiosity landed me into something other than trouble, huh?"

"You've given my father his spark of life back. All he's ever wanted is to take care of his family. Now he's got a way to do that."

Honorable men. Both father and son.

His gaze intensified. "What my momma said, about staying around. Any hope in that?"

What was he saying?

He reached for her hands and tugged her closer. "I'd like you to."

She searched his eyes. Though she longed with everything in her to say yes, she needed more than that.

"I love you, Faith. I have since you first drove into town."

"Since your tire crashed into me, you mean?"

He laughed. "Yeah. Since then."

"I suppose that's one way to get a girl."

"Did it work?"

Could she trust him? Not just to say these things, even feel these things now, but to stick around even when life got hard? To protect her heart, should she give it, fully, to him?

"I've never felt this way about a woman before. Except…"

With Lydia. The woman he'd held tight to, till they'd parted at death.

Drake wasn't like the other men she'd dated. He wasn't the walk-away kind. And if everything she'd witnessed proved anything, she knew he wasn't the type to say meaningless sweet nothings, either.

She belonged here, with him.

She'd call Toni in the morning. She wasn't

comfortable being a full-on partner, especially considering she had zero to invest. But she'd love to have her artwork displayed. Toni would do that, and in return, Faith would give her the loudest and most frequent Facebook shout-outs ever.

And a mention in that feature Lone Star Gems had promised to write—now that they knew the story behind the church, including the romantic way Faith had uncovered it.

"I believe you," she said. "And I…" She took a deep breath. She could trust him. "I love you, too."

He gave a whoop and pulled her close and planted a kiss on her mouth. She melted against him.

She loved this cowboy. As much as she'd fought against it, he'd stolen her heart completely.

He pulled away, leaving her breathless, and quirked an eyebrow at her. "Does that mean you're staying?"

"I guess it does."

"Yeehaw!" She startled at the sound of Elizabeth's voice, and turned to find her watching the two of them. Her friend spun around. "Momma, we best start clearing out the guest room tonight. Because Faith is in the house!"

Epilogue

Faith ran her hands down the smooth satin of her gown, her stomach as jittery as her heart was full. She could hardly believe this day had come, that she was here on Drake's ranch, that he'd chosen her. Not just for today, not just for a romantic horse ride or a twirl around the dance floor, but to be his forever.

Best of all, both her parents were here and were managing to get along. She cast a glance toward her father, scrolling through his phone a few feet away. He might appear disinterested to some, but that was how he always acted when nervous.

When he looked up, she smiled, hoping to convey how much his presence meant to her. And her mom… She was likely back in the bathroom for the third time that morning. Nerves.

"Ms. Faith!" William burst into the tent, his cheeks red and puffy. Sweat slicked his blond hair to his forehead. He held out a handful of dandelions and bluebonnets, likely picked from the pasture.

She exchanged a smile with Toni, her bridesmaid, then lowered herself to William's eye level. "Thank you. These are beautiful." She took the flowers and kissed his forehead.

"There you are!" Mrs. Owens entered with a huff, her face more flushed than her grandson's, as if she'd been chasing after him for some time. "You're going to get your clothes all messed up." Her gaze landed on Faith, and she paused with a hand to her neck. "Such a beautiful girl. Inside and out. Drake is lucky to have you." She grabbed Faith's hands and kissed her cheek.

"Now to corral this little guy and get him where he needs to be." Mrs. Owens placed her palms on William's shoulders and turned him toward the canopy exit. "He seems to be taking his role as flower boy quite seriously."

Faith laughed. "Where's Trevor?"

"With Papa Owens, where he's supposed to be." She gave William a stern look, then shifted to Faith with a smile. "See you soon." With a wave, she left.

Toni took a swig from her water bottle. "You nervous?"

"About tripping, yes." The potential hazard of

having an outdoor wedding. Faith poked her head out and watched as families filled the chairs arranged in the meadow. The bluebonnets, sprinkled throughout red and yellow flowers, swayed in the breeze, and the chirping of birds harmonized with the melody of Elizabeth's harp.

The tempo changed, and Toni bounced on the balls of her feet. "It's time, girlfriend."

Faith nodded and watched as Drake emerged from the stables and made his way toward the rustic altar. Though his boots and Stetson contrasted sharply with his tuxedo, combined they fit her cowboy, and the surroundings, well.

The rest of the wedding party, a handful of Faith and Drake's closest friends, and his boys, followed.

Her dad came to her side. "We're up, baby girl."

A lump lodged in her throat. He hadn't called her that since the day she left for college. She gave a slight nod, then looped her arm through his. Walking carefully to avoid stumbling over the uneven grass in her two-inch heels, she let her father lead her out of the tent and down the aisle.

When Drake's gaze captured hers, her thoughts narrowed to one thing: she loved that man. With everything in her.

Drake's breath caught as his beautiful bride glided toward him in a simple yet elegant dress.

She wore her hair pulled back, with wisps of curls framing her oval face. The way she peered up at him—shyly, almost demurely—accelerated his pulse.

It took all his self-control not to draw her close and kiss her right then and there.

Pastor Roger's voice, talking about the sacred union between a husband and wife, drifted to the background as thoughts of a life spent with Faith filled Drake's mind. Images of her sitting on his rocker reading stories to his boys. Of all of them gathered around the dinner table, her sweet laugh filling the room. Of waking up to see her lying next to him, no makeup on, hair mussed, eyes filled with the same love and passion with which she looked at him now.

"Drake?"

"Huh?" He startled and turned to the pastor.

"Do you take Faith to be your lawfully wedded wife? To love, cherish and support, through church fires, barn dances and broken dishwashers?"

He chuckled, then sobered, his eyes on her. "I do." Trevor produced the ring, and Drake took her trembling hand in his and slid it on her finger.

"And do you, Faith Nichols, take Drake Owens to be your lawfully wedded husband? To love, respect and encourage through rained-out projects, runaway heifers and…" He eyed William, who'd plopped onto the ground and was searching through the blades of grass, most likely for a bug of some sort. "...rambunctious little ones, from this day forward?"

"I do." A single tear slid from her eye and followed the soft contours of her cheek.

Drake thumbed it away and let her slip the gold band on his finger.

"Then by the powers vested in me, and with the blessings of all the fine folks here..."

Someone whistled, and a deep-throated voice called out, "You got that right!"

"...I now pronounce you husband and wife."

Drake whooped, pumped his fist, then pulled her close, kissing her like a man who'd been waiting months for this moment.

The day when his sweet Faith would be his.

* * * * *

If you loved this story by Jennifer Slattery, pick up these other Love Inspired books:

His Wyoming Baby Blessing *by Jill Kemerer*
Her Twins' Cowboy Dad *by Patricia Johns*
The Rancher's Redemption *by Myra Johnson*

Available now from Love Inspired!

Find more great reads at LoveInspired.com

Dear Reader,

The backdrop of this story emerged one day when I encountered an article about the historic Painted Churches of Texas. Though I don't have an artistic bone in my body, I have great admiration for those gifted with such creativity and skill. It might not surprise you, then, that I received great enjoyment from writing Faith's story as she works with all three mediums—and more!

My most enjoyable experience, however, came while researching the processes related to stained glass artwork. Through an Internet search, I discovered a stained glass store about an hour away that teaches patrons how to cut and design stained glass. I immediately signed my daughter and I up, and together we spent seven Saturdays cutting glass, and finding much to laugh about—often due to my frequent mistakes! I was also able to ask the staff at Architectural Glassarts all my story-related questions regarding the restoration of historic stained glass windows like those Faith encountered.

Each window, with its unique and perhaps even jagged pieces, reminds me of the beauty available through community. We're all different, and we all have our rough edges and chipped areas. Our individual colors are unique and vibrant, but when we come together, learn to lean on one another, and support each other, as Sage Creek residents do, we become a beautiful tapestry that reveals God's love and grace.

May we each find our place in such a life-giving community.

Jennifer

Get 4 FREE REWARDS!

We'll send you 2 FREE Books plus 2 FREE Mystery Gifts.

Love Inspired® Suspense books feature Christian characters facing challenges to their faith... and lives.

FREE Value Over **$20**

Get 4 FREE REWARDS!

We'll send you 2 FREE Books plus 2 FREE Mystery Gifts.

Harlequin® Heartwarming™ Larger-Print books feature traditional values of home, family, community and—most of all—love.

FREE Value Over **$20**
